LOVE IN RUINS

Also by Auriane Desombre

For Young Adults

I Love You S'More

I Think I Love You

For Middle Graders

The Sister Split

LOVE IN RUINS

AURIANE DESOMBRE

Delacorte
Romance

Delacorte Romance
An imprint of Random House Children's Books
A division of Penguin Random House LLC
1745 Broadway, New York, NY 10019
penguinrandomhouse.com
getunderlined.com

Editor: Kelsey Horton
Cover Designer: Trisha Previte
Interior Designer: Cathy Bobak
Production Editor: Jamie Johnson
Managing Editor: Tamar Schwartz
Production Manager: Liz Sutton

Library of Congress Cataloging-in-Publication Data is available upon request.
ISBN 978-0-593-80758-3 (trade pbk.) — ISBN 978-0-593-80760-6 (ebook)

The text of this book is set in 11.3-point Warnock Pro.
Notepaper art by LinaTruman/stock.adobe.com
Greek poster art background by hadeev/stock.adobe.com
Classic Greek key border by Ana Lo/stock.adobe.com

Manufactured in the United States of America
1st Printing

The authorized representative in the EU for product safety and compliance is
Penguin Random House Ireland, Morrison Chambers, 32 Nassau Street,
Dublin D02 YH68, Ireland, https://eu-contact.penguin.ie.

For Erin, who lights up and steadies my world.
You could definitely beat me in a footrace.

CHAPTER ONE

I'M JUST STEPPING OFF A PLANE, but it feels like I'm throwing myself off a precipice. My whole life—at least, from the moment I got my five-year-old hands on the pages of *D'Aulaires' Book of Greek Myths*—has been building toward this moment. Now that it's finally here, my primary emotion is sheer exhaustion. Momentous life moments simply should not happen right after ten hours of sitting upright in the world's smallest chair.

Liam bumps against my shoulder as we follow Ms. Barlowe down the Jetway to customs. I would be well cast in "The Princess and the Pea," but he has the magical ability to fall asleep anywhere. The pep in his step is absurd.

"Can you believe we're here?" he asks, hoisting his duffel higher across his shoulder.

"Honestly?" I look around the customs line. We're surrounded by gray walls, fluorescent lighting, and a blue carpet underfoot, thick with dirt. The view from the large windows gives out onto nothing but an airplane parking lot. Airports are too stuck out of time for the moment to sink in, even with the Greek letters printed on every sign. "It doesn't feel real."

Most of our cohort seems to feel similarly. George is staring through the winding customs line as if the room were empty, and Bodhi stands next to him with equally vacant eyes. Amalia is practically asleep on Lucy's shoulder. Henry's yawns are so huge, I can see straight to his tonsils. Liam and Ms. Barlowe are the only ones who seem capable of registering their surroundings.

"That's what you get for watching *Mamma Mia! Here We Go Again* instead of sleeping on the plane," Liam tells me.

I flick him lightly on the temple. "Don't disrespect *Mamma Mia! Here We Go Again* like that. It's art. And I wouldn't have been able to sleep, anyway."

The toddler behind me saw to *that*. Not that I begrudge him the two a.m. sobfest. Kids have just as much of a right to be on a plane or any public space as adults do, and they're allowed to do normal kid things like cry when there's turbulence. But I'm an insomniac in the best conditions. Spotify crowns me as a proud top 1 percent listener of "10 Hours Air Conditioner Noises" every year for a reason.

Despite my exhaustion making time feel stretchy and slow, I make it to the front of the line, the customs officer approves me, and I follow the group to baggage claim. There are seven of us in total, plus Ms. Barlowe. The eight biggest nerds in our school. The only ones not just willing but desperate to give up a free pe-

riod every day to study classics. Once a day we meet in Ms. Barlowe's tiny classroom to throw ourselves into the ancient world
and everything it has to offer. And now, thanks to Ms. Barlowe
winning a grant from some fancy teacher fellowship program,
we're spending a month of our summer break in actual Greece.

Even though I'm here, staring at the baggage claim car-
ousel and waiting for my blue sticker-covered suitcase to ap-
pear, I can't wrap my head around it. I'm in Greece. My first
time out of New York City, and it's to actual, real-life, where-
the-myths-originated *Greece*. I keep repeating it in my head,
hoping it will sink in.

I connect to the airport Wi-Fi after successfully guessing
which Greek-lettered buttons to click on, and my phone immediately lights up with a billion notifications. I ignore the ones
from the family group chat, which might as well be renamed
"Lizzie's Wedding Planning Committee, Where We Only Care
About Weddings" at this point, and swipe to the classics cohort's group chat instead.

No-Murder Secret History

LUCY: i am so tired

AMALIA: we are all standing next to you

LUCY: simply too tired to talk

HENRY: FAIR

"Not fair," Liam teases, grinning as he nudges Lucy. "We're *here*. Wake *up*."

"Need bus nap," Lucy groans, tipping her head onto Henry's shoulder. He pats her thick brown curls.

Liam yanks his falling-apart notebook out of his backpack and flips through it. Every page is covered in tiny penciled notes all crammed together, his thoughts so piled on top of one another that they are unintelligible to anyone but him. It's my favorite thing he owns, because it feels like a map of his brain, all interconnected thoughts and overlapping sentences, an appearance of scatterbrained energy that still isn't enough to hide the brilliance beneath. He stops when he gets to an uncharacteristically neat numbered list.

"Okay," he says, tilting the page toward me. "Our Grecian bucket list. I've already added *steal a boat, visit the ruins at night*, and *find a secret beach*. Anything you want to add?"

"I have some I wanna remove," I say, eyeing the first item on his list.

He circles *steal a boat* twice. "Not, like, *steal* steal. But we simply must find ourselves on a boat at some point this summer."

Can't argue with that. I take his notebook—I'm the only one aside from him who's allowed to hold it—and examine the list more closely. Before he can stop me, I add *go to Delos* in pen. It's Artemis's birthplace, and there's no way I'm coming all the way here just to miss it. He nods in approval when I hand the notebook back to him. He knows better than anyone that I was practically born with an Artemis obsession stamped into my DNA. When I look back, my obsession with the goddess of the moon and hunt was baby's first sign of lesbianism.

Well, that and my very transparent crush on Katara. My lifelong love for *Avatar: The Last Airbender* has always had an agenda.

"This is going to be the best summer ever," Liam says as he snaps the notebook shut. His tone is ironic; he's painfully aware that he sounds like he's reading a cheesy line of dialogue from an old straight-to-TV teen movie, but I can tell that the sentiment behind the words is real. I squeeze his hand in agreement.

"It will be."

Once we all have our bags, Ms. Barlowe leads us toward the sliding doors to the pickup area. A handful of people mill around on the other side of the doors, some holding signs welcoming relatives or offering overpriced taxi services, and as we walk through the doors to the passenger pickup area, everyone swivels our way to see if their arrival is about to emerge. Most people look away again when they register us, going back to searching for whoever they're here to pick up, but a tall brunette woman rushes toward the door to greet us.

"Welcome to Greece," Ms. Galanis says, throwing her arms around Ms. Barlowe's shoulders. "I can't believe you're here."

Ms. Galanis is our fellowship-funded Greek educator. We've met with her on Zoom once a week this year, and all of us have multiple notebooks filled to the brim with everything she's taught us in preparation for our trip.

"We're so excited," Ms. Barlowe says, glancing around. Even though we're still at the airport and in that this-could-be-anywhere feeling, the Greek language explodes around us in cries of welcome as people in the crowd recognize loved ones coming through the doors. It's starting to make it all feel a little more real. "I can't believe we're actually here. Is your daughter still joining us?"

"Of course," Ms. Galanis says with a smile. "She'd never pass up the opportunity for a free trip around the country."

Our two teachers turn to us, beaming. I can't believe Ms. Barlowe has enough in her to maintain her usual level of sunshine energy.

"Our bus will be meeting us in the back parking lot, so you'll have to lug your suitcases for a bit," Ms. Galanis says apologetically. "My daughter, Melanie, is going to join us for the trip and for the . . . Well, I'll let Ms. Barlowe do the honors when we get on the bus."

They exchange winks, and I glance at Liam. He shrugs back at me. What have they concocted for us now?

"Regardless, she'll meet us at our first stop in Syntagma Square," Ms. Galanis says, gesturing toward the airport doors. "Shall we?"

We walk out of the airport and drag our suitcases down the sidewalk. It's only midmorning, but the summer sun has already warmed the air. A trickle of sweat forms on my neck, and not for the first time, I wish that our itinerary allowed for a shower stop before we begin our first day of sightseeing.

Still, even though all I've seen of Greece so far is the flat gray concrete of this parking lot surrounded by thick-leaved shrubs, I'm already in love.

In spite of the sweaty conditions, we make it to the bus, which is parked along the curb, storage doors open to greet us. The driver introduces herself as Kendra and helps us load our bags into the bus's storage area before we all find our seats.

Ms. Barlowe warned us an alarming number of times that we simply *had* to sleep on the plane because we would be arriving to a full day of activities whether we were well rested or not. But as exhausted as I am after ignoring her advice, there's no way I can try to catch up with a nap on the bus. Liam and I find seats near the front, and from the moment the bus pulls out of the airport, I'm glued to the window.

I'm 4,921 miles away from my home in New York. That's the farthest away I've ever been, and right now that feels pretty good. Between Lizzie yapping about nothing but her wedding, Andrea invading every space of the home with her leaving-for-college prep, and my parents only taking a break from either to ask me pointed questions like *How was therapy this week, Natalie?*, I can use all that space and more. Especially if the other end is the site of my dreams.

Our bus barrels down the curved highway, and as we emerge from a tunnel, Mount Hymettus bursts into view, its greenery punctuated by the white slate of rocky paths. White buildings crowd the landscape below it. Athens unfurls in front of our eyes as we trundle down each bend in the road.

Even from a distance, the view promises the bustle of a modern city exploding around its ancient roots. I'm too far away to make out any details, but I can spot the central hill on which the ancient Acropolis has been resting for thousands of years, surveying the landscape that has changed so much around it. Today it's surrounded by a crowded sprawl of apartments and office buildings. And it finally sinks in. After years of studying the ancient beginnings of this place—the language, culture, literature, art, and philosophy of this land—I'm actually *here*.

What better escape is there?

The traffic around Syntagma Square might be the most chaotic driving I've ever witnessed, and that's really saying something, as all the driving I've seen to date has taken place in New York City. The bus swerves and lurches as a zillion cars and motorcycles leapfrog around us. Car horns and overlapping voices shout through the street. I'm not prone to motion sickness, but I find myself desperately scanning the horizon to stave off the carsick feeling brewing in my guts as Kendra careens into a narrow, cobblestone-paved side street.

Mercifully, we stop here.

Ms. Barlowe grips the back of her seat to stand shakily in the aisle. The bus comes with a rickety microphone that sends a screech of feedback through the bus. We all cringe alert, and Ms. Barlowe flashes us an evil grin as she stows the microphone back into its port behind the driver.

"You'll just have to listen closely," she half shouts in that teacher-projection kind of way. "We're here at our first stop. We're going to tour Syntagma Square with Ms. Galanis and her daughter, Melanie, who will be joining our trip, and then we will be benevolent rulers and free you for lunch and shopping in the surrounding area."

From the back of the bus, Lucy cheers. She's been ready and waiting for her first Greek meal since the moment we found out about the trip.

"But first," Ms. Barlowe goes on, smoothly ignoring Lucy, "I have an exciting announcement."

We all sit up a little straighter. The last time she had an exciting announcement, we found out we were spending half our summer break in Greece.

"As you know, part of this summer will be spent researching and working on your special projects," Ms. Barlowe says.

Liam and I exchange excited looks. Given that our cohort includes the eight biggest nerds in the school, we're all actually excited about our projects. As soon as she found out about the trip, Ms. Barlowe designed an open-ended assignment to let us research any aspect of ancient Greece we want and present our findings however we decide. It feels like the most grown-up, academia-y project I've ever gotten to do in school. Plus, I finally get an outlet for all my research into the stories and myths about the followers of Artemis.

Liam is already deep into his project. He's incorporating his research on the Battle of Marathon into a novel in verse.

His drafts of the opening pages are stunning, and I'm already obsessed with them. And not just because, as one of the fastest girls on the school's track team, I've been his main source for "what running feels like." Even Liam has boundaries he will not cross in the name of research, and exercising outside of the school's pool is one of them.

I have no vision for my project. Just a heart full of love for Artemis (and four notebooks full of research).

"The Stephen Goddard Research Institute Fund for Precollegiate Scholarship." Ms. Barlowe pauses. "Phew. The guys who gave us the money to come here have developed an academic decathlon, in which you're all invited to compete. There will be ten events, your special projects being one. The rest range from academic challenges like speech and debate to summer-camp fun along the lines of scavenger hunts and talent shows. In addition to the money to come here, these guys also gave us prize money totaling five thousand dollars, to be awarded to the student who wins the most points in this summerlong decathlon."

There's a pause, and then the bus explodes into a cacophony of questions.

"When's the deadline?" Amalia asks. She's scribbling in her notebook, and she's somehow already developed a color code.

"Can we still present our research any way we want for the project piece?" Henry asks. He's a rising senior in AP Drawing and has been working on a series of oil paintings starring people of color from Greek myths.

"No way you're changing your project," Bodhi tells him, waving his shaggy brown hair out of his eyes. "It's your masterpiece."

Liam, ever the *pleasure to have in class* from his elementary school days, raises his hand.

"Can I change my topic?" George yells from his seat next to Lucy. "Nothing about the Trojan War is winning originality points."

"You should still let yourself be guided by your passions," Ms. Galanis says, and Ms. Barlowe nods heartily.

"You'll be working on these projects for the month in addition to all the work you've already put in," she reminds us. "It will be difficult work, and you'll need your passion to pull you through the tough moments."

"Do we have to enter?" That last one comes from me, and the bus falls eerily quiet as everyone stops to stare.

"Why wouldn't we?" George asks. "We have to do the work for our projects, anyway. Might as well try for some prize money."

It's true that five thousand dollars could take me a long way. It's enough to bring me back here later on in my high school career, when I've had more time to study the classics. It's enough to plan a year's worth of visits to Andrea at UCLA without my parents in tow. It's enough to justify cutting down on my hours at my part-time job scooping gelato and to buy back some of my Friday nights.

But the thought of competition is also enough to send me spiraling. I'm the only freshman in this program. Liam and

Amalia are the only sophomores. Everyone else is a junior or a recently graduated senior, with a billion AP classes and advanced projects under their belts already. What chance do my subpar research and childhood love of Artemis stand against Henry's art talent or Liam's collegiate writing skills?

I didn't come here to spend the summer worrying about not being good enough.

"It's not mandatory," Ms. Barlowe says. Her eyes meet mine, and she squints at me through the thin frames of her glasses, as if trying to read me. "But we'll encourage all of you to go for it."

I nod. The only thing scarier than competition is disappointing Ms. Barlowe. She's my favorite teacher, and she took a huge leap of faith by letting me into the program in my freshman year based on my eighth-grade report card and the impassioned essay about the female goddesses I submitted alongside my application. It's been the main goal of my year to prove to her that she made the right decision. She loved my midterm project about Anne Carson's take on Hercules. Letting her down now that I've finally made it to a rising sophomore is a terrifying thought.

But the brain gremlin is starting up its favorite tap dance. *You're not good enough for this. If you enter this competition, all you'll do is prove that to everyone else.*

"We'll have more time to go over the project and answer all your questions at the hotel tonight," Ms. Barlowe says. "For now, let's get off this bus and into Athens!"

Everyone cheers, and even I muster up a whoop through

the thick fog that has mercilessly descended upon my thoughts. We move to gather our things, the bus aisle growing thick with backpacks and totes as everyone files toward the doors. I follow Liam, and my feet finally land on the sidewalks of Athens.

Being a pedestrian in Syntagma is just as chaotic as being a car passenger. The crowds walk thickly on the sidewalk, in the street—everywhere, it seems, is fair game for a throng of people to amass. Syntagma Square is the city center of Athens. A huge paved square sits in the middle of the busy intersecting streets. It's looked over by the impressive Hellenic Parliament, an imposing building with walls the color of faded sunlight and a set of Ionic columns across the entrance. The smell of fresh-cut greenery mixes with the spiced scents steaming from the street food vendors lined along the sides of the square. Every corner of the square is bursting with color and sound—the shouts of people calling to one another, the screech of tires coming too fast around the bend, the spray of water hitting the sides of the fountain that sits in the middle of the square.

It's my first glimpse of Athens up close, and I love it here already.

As we all know and as Ms. Barlowe reminds us while we make our way toward the parliament building, it was built in the 1830s and '40s as the royal palace for King Otto and now serves as the home of Parliament and the Senate. Before it stands the Tomb of the Unknown Soldier, a cenotaph war memorial watched over by the Evzones guards.

"And don't worry, we did time this right," Ms. Barlowe says with a grin. "In just a few minutes, we'll see the changing of the guard."

Lucy lets out a quiet cheer. She's made us watch countless videos of the guards changing, and we've always willingly joined in on her obsession. The ceremony is beyond impressive, and I'm struck by the guards' total concentration. They seem oblivious to the crowd of onlookers, their focus devoted first to the movement and then to the stillness of their task.

I've never managed to be that focused on anything. It seems like there's a dance of intrusive thoughts always ready to break out, always simmering in the back of my mind, no matter how immersed I wish I could be in the moment.

Even now as I gather with my cohort on the wide sidewalk in front of the building, only half of me is watching when we all crane our necks to catch our first glimpse of the coming guards. A group marching in two lines appears around the corner. Only two will ultimately stay to watch over the tomb and the square, but the change itself is a group affair: the guards, the audience, and the billion thoughts tap-dancing so loudly in my brain that I can barely hear the rhythmic click of the guards' shoes as they stop in front of the tomb.

My classmates seem to have no trouble forgetting about the competition for now. Amalia is still scribbling in her notebook. Lucy is filming the three guards walking up to the tomb—two to take their places for the next hour, and one acting as the supervisor of the change—their legs extending with each step in the traditional movement for this moment. Liam's eyes are huge, as if he can't stand to even blink.

I'm technically looking at the guards, but I'm only half seeing them. My thoughts are tangible enough that they cloud my vision. Or maybe it's that they're sucking me so far back into my brain that I'm not really *here* anymore. I'm trapped in the coils of my thoughts, forced to play out the scenario the brain gremlin has invented for me today.

You're going to do so bad on your project that the institute's judging panel will recommend Ms. Barlowe dismiss you from the program. And then Liam won't want to be your friend anymore because you won't be in the same program together. And then you'll be alone.

The two guards being relieved have made it back to the group, and the guards taking their places stand still at their posts on opposite sides of the tomb.

"It must be so hard to stand that still for an hour," Liam breathes next to me.

I nod. I can't fathom that kind of stillness, but I yearn for it. Being still in the moment, letting my surroundings take precedence over the slithering mass of thoughts always threatening to pull me deeper into the recesses of my writhing brain—that sounds like a kind of freedom I've never had.

If you don't enter the contest, Ms. Barlowe will think you're not serious about your work. And then she'll dismiss you from the program. And Liam won't want to be your friend anymore, and you'll be alone.

Paige, the therapist my parents made me start seeing, recently named the gremlin OCD. But I've been living with it my whole life. Paige just met me a few months ago. What the hell does she know?

It's not like I'm germophobic, nor do I count things. Paige is completely wrong on this one. Everyone worries sometimes. That's just part of the human experience.

The only way to not end up alone is to do a perfect job on this project. Win the decathlon.

The group of guards marches back down the street, leaving the two by the tomb to their work. Some of the crowd burst into appreciative applause as they round the corner, out of sight.

Ms. Barlowe launches into an explanation about the history of the guard, which I barely listen to. I've started back at the beginning of this thought circle, like my brain is a dog chasing its own tail. Hyperfocused on its mission, with the end goal always out of reach. Our cohort starts drifting away from her, and that's when I realize we've been dismissed to Ermou Street for lunch and shopping.

"I will be having a gyro, and none of you can stop me," Lucy informs us. "But you're welcome to join."

We all take her up on it, partially because a gyro sounds amazing right now and partially because splitting up in this lively crowd sounds more intimidating than any of us can handle just a few hours into the trip. Lucy has no more idea where she's going than the rest of us, but somehow she leads us to a small restaurant that smells like it invented the concept of food.

"Mia píta gýro chorís tyrí parakaló," I say when it's my turn to order. *Without cheese, please* is the first thing I learned how to say in Greek when I found out we were coming here. It's the one place culinarily where I draw the line.

"Chorís tyrí?"

I start as I turn to meet the warm brown eyes of the girl in line behind me. She's tall, so much so that I have to tilt my head back to take in her expression even though I'm not short myself. In a perfect Greek accent, she repeats my stumbled-through words, her lips popping at the ends of her words, and I want to melt into the honeyed curves of her syllables.

"That's practically sacrilege," she says in smooth English, correctly clocking from my accent that the rest of the conversation can't be in Greek if it has any hope of survival.

"I fear I'm not a cheese girlie," I admit. Against my better judgment, I find myself racking my brain for something—anything—else to say. There's something so easy about this girl's smile, the way it lights up her face. I'm drawn in by the warmth of her, and even though I'm usually way too awkward for small talk with strangers, I don't want this particular moment to end.

"To each their own," she says with a grin. Before I can come up with something sufficiently witty, the cashier rattles off an amount in Greek, and I find myself scrambling to read his handwriting on his notepad to figure out how much I owe.

I navigate paying with the unfamiliar currency, and by the time I'm done, the girl is gone. I sigh, letting my fingers close around the warm foil wrapping my pita. Even through the packaging, I can feel the doughy softness of the bread. It'll have to be enough to soothe the bittersweet ache that comes with the yearning for a connection that's now been missed.

Resisting the urge to down the pita before I've even left the line, I join the cohort outside. We all take our first bites together, and I immediately rank this as among the best lunches of my life. The gyro seems like it should be simple—pork, roasted on a rotating spit, tucked into the pita with tzatziki, tomatoes, fries, and a gorgeous absence of cheese—but it melts together into the perfect meal. The right amount of grease sizzles against the crispiness of the meat, the tang of the tzatziki spicing up the crisp doughiness of the fries. I could write books of love poems about this wrap and never run out of flowery metaphors to tell it how much I've fallen in love. It's almost enough to make up for the loss of the girl's warm brown eyes smiling down into mine.

"I want to cry," Lucy says. "Just knowing this can't last forever is the saddest thing that's ever happened to me."

"I'm getting another one." George finished his in three bites and, true to his word, is back in the line immediately.

"I'm so full," Lucy says, looking after him yearningly. Then she sighs. "But my time here is so limited."

And with that, she joins George. Liam laughs.

"I love them so much."

I'm halfway through my wrap, and the edge of my hunger

has been sated enough that I find my eyes wandering around the square, scanning against my will for another glimpse of the girl. I can't help myself—when it comes to impossible connections that have no hope of turning into anything real, I turn into a puddle of yearning, romantic goo. It's only when a crush could potentially be requited that it turns into something sharp and scary, to be handled with ginger delicacy.

But now that I'll never see this girl again, what's to stop me from imagining our entire future together unfurling under this hot summer sun? Our hands growing sweaty as our fingers intertwine, neither of us caring. Laughing together on a beach somewhere, our gradual sunburns going unnoticed because we can't look away from each other's eyes. Kissing the warmth of her smile . . .

Of course, she's nowhere to be found. And even if she were, she'd be kept a safe distance away, a stranger passing by on the street. I give up my search and finish my wrap as George and Lucy return with their fresh hauls.

Eventually Lucy's fears come to pass, and we all finish our lunches. She perks up when she remembers that we still have an hour to wander Ermou Street, taking in the sights of the fancy Hotel Grande Bretagne and animated bars and cafes lining the street. We walk down the cobblestoned street together, our voices overlapping as we discuss the month ahead.

"We have to make this the best month of our lives, guys," Lucy says. She's one of the recently graduated seniors, and she's spent the last few summers working as a camp counselor. When it comes to summertime fun, she's the undisputed leader of our group. "I'm thinking we go through the itinerary and add our own spice to every event."

Spice sounds scary, but I let her go on.

"I'm talking side quests, I'm talking summer romances, I'm talking a fabulous end-of-trip party to celebrate this high-light of our young lives."

My heart sinks, and acid floods my chest. Why do we have to bring romance into it? Contrary to popular belief, summer is a decidedly unromantic time. It's sweaty, it's humid, and it smells like sunscreen. What about all that screams *Get it on*? I can feel blotches of red staining my pale neck and cheeks. Looking yearningly for a girl from a gyro line is one thing, but actively seeking a real romance is another matter entirely. One that comes with the mortifying ordeal of being known. Simply not for me, thanks.

But Lucy points right at me as she continues. "I mean it. Romance for all. I did not come all the way here not to have a fling with a Greek boy."

"Me neither," Bodhi agrees.

I look to Liam for help, but he provides none. "It's low stakes," he says to me quietly. "Just fun. It's okay to let yourself have that. This is all literally hypothetical."

"Easy for you to say." I give him a murderous glare. He's not the one whose brain clams up every time someone gets too close to knowing how it ticks. What does he know about the fears that crawl in relentless, spiderlike tendrils through me, dictating all the choices I make? "I just don't want to date anyone. Why can't you accept that?"

He sighs. "Because I can see you do. You're just standing in your own way."

This sounds like something Paige would say, so I give myself permission to ignore it. Indulging in the fantasy of a pretend summer fling is enough. Letting anything become real means involving the brain gremlin, and no one needs that.

"Shouldn't we be focusing on our projects?" I ask the wider group, trying to appeal to everyone's inner nerd.

"I can write love poetry and still find a hot summer boyfriend," Bodhi assures me. "In fact, I'm sure the poetry will help."

This is fair. His talent is beyond. Anyone who reads his work is bound to fall at least a little in love with him.

I shrug. "I'll be focusing on my project."

Lucy grins as she puts an arm around my shoulders. "Spoken like a true follower of Artemis."

"Spoken like a true coward," Liam adds, low enough that only I can hear.

I roll my eyes, but at least the group drops it as we make our way down the square. I refuse to give in to any of their nonsense. The only way I'm going to make it to next year is if I create a good-enough project, one that proves my worth. Which means I need to give it my full focus.

No matter what.

At least, that's what I tell myself. But when we make it back to the bus after our hour of wandering, weighed down with shopping bags (everyone else) and needless worries (me), she's there. The girl from the gyro line.

Standing by the open door of the bus, tanned arms folded across her chest, that warm smile lighting up her face as she talks to Ms. Barlowe.

"Welcome back," Ms. Galanis tells us as we reach the bus. "I'm delighted to introduce you all to my daughter, Melanie."

She gestures to Gyro Line Girl, and I might as well go straight into cardiac arrest given the way my heart explodes into a flurry of beats, bleeding one into the next. Melanie's eyes sweep over the group, blinking in recognition when they land on me.

"Chorís tyrí," she says, smiling at me. "We meet again."

I can't even try to come up with something witty this time. I'm in too much shock. This girl, the one I let myself look for, is joining us all summer? With her distracting tallness and gooey smile and honeyed eyes?

If I let myself yearn before, it's paled in comparison to the reality of this moment. Because this could all be possible now. With the time ahead of us, all the things I let myself dream about—our hands, our eyes, our lips—could become true.

But now that I'm waking up into it, it doesn't feel like a dream anymore. The yearning curdles into a cold sweat that ticks down the back of my neck, and I drop my gaze to an old piece of gum congealing on the pavement. This has turned so fast into something to be afraid of, to run from. The brain gremlin tap-dances away, reminding me of all the fears that would come true if I ever let someone know me enough to love me. Because I'm sufficiently messed up that I know that seeing me could never lead to loving me. So instead of uttering any of the smooth one-liners I might've used in my fantasy of how this summer could've played out between Hot Gyro Girl and me, I smile politely at the reality of Melanie as I quickly push past her to make my way after Liam, back onto the bus.

Nancy Barlowe's Classics and the Ancient World Cohort
Greece Through an Ancient Lens Tour
Summer Decathlon

Our decathlon combines teamwork, individual scholarship, and a healthy dose of summer fun. To be completed over the course of the summer tour, with scheduling at the discretion of the faculty chaperones, this competition invites all participating students to deepen their knowledge and immersion into the world of ancient Greece.

1. Final project abstract (5 points)
2. Scavenger hunt (5 points)
3. Open mic night/ancient talent show (5 points)
4. Art show (5 points)
5. Speech/performance (10 points)
6. Beach games (5 points)
7. Debate (10 points)
8. Trivia competition (10 points)
9. Olympic games (5 points)
10. Final project (40 points)

The winner(s) of the final projects and abstracts will be determined by a panel of judges appointed by the Stephen Goddard Research Institute Fund for Precollegiate Scholarship.

The winner(s) of the remaining events will be determined by the faculty chaperones of the tour, using criteria outlined by the Stephen Goddard Research Institute Fund for Precollegiate Scholarship.

The winner of the decathlon will be determined by final point totals and will be awarded a grand prize of five thousand dollars.

Participation is not a mandatory requirement of attendance on the tour.

CHAPTER TWO

IT TOOK A FAIR AMOUNT OF begging and parental intervention, but the school agreed to let me and Liam be roommates for the trip. It's pure heteronormative nonsense that the school ever questioned it for a second. Why *wouldn't* a gay guy and a lesbian be allowed to room together? But the administration finally got their thinking caps on right and let it happen. We had to promise to be on our best behavior the whole time, which we fully intend to do.

Minus right now, of course.

"So, where are we going?" I ask.

"Give me a *moment*," Liam snarls, tossing a T-shirt out of his suitcase.

We checked in about ten seconds ago, and Liam has already destroyed our little hotel room. The area around his twin bed is littered with all his clothes, which he's tearing out of his suitcase piece by piece in search of the perfect outfit for our first night of sneaking out.

I peer out the window onto the busy street where we're staying. The exhaustion I've been lugging around all day has evaporated, my body comfortable in the knowledge that it's five p.m. in New York right now.

Of course, it's midnight here, and our wake-up call is a mere six hours away. But the restaurant across the street stays open all night, and the jet lag has my stomach rumbling even after our copious dinner.

And, well, who am I to argue with that?

So here I am in one of the nicer sundresses I brought, a strappy yellow situation with flowers that Lizzie embroidered on the hem. I finally got to wash the plane out of my hair, and I decide I have time to curl it a little while Liam finds the right shirt for the night.

When he decides on a blue button-down and I accept that my brown frizz is as good as it's going to get, we poke our heads out the hotel room door. The hallway is empty. Ms. Barlowe is surely fast asleep by now. She extolled the virtues of melatonin far too much to be a woman awake past the ten p.m. lights-out announcement. All the same, we tiptoe our way to the elevator.

"I'd take the stairs to the side entrance if I were you."

I almost start out of my skin. We whirl around to find Melanie smirking at us, her arms crossed.

"My mom and your teacher have discovered the joys of

the hotel bar," she warns us. "They'll see you walk out if you go through the lobby."

"Thanks," I say, staring at my shoelaces. There's a splotch of paint on my right shoe that must've been there since a teaching artist came to lead our cohort in a demo on painting vases.

"Wanna come with us?" Liam asks. The effort not to roll my eyes at him physically hurts.

"Where are you going?"

"That restaurant we saw across the street," I tell her. I have to fight the urge to blush every time I meet her eyes, so I stick to examining my shoelaces as I talk. "A midnight snack was calling to me."

She grins. "I can show you somewhere better."

And that's how we end up on a rooftop terrace overlooking the literal Acropolis. It's my first time ever seeing it, and I'll admit, I tear up at the sight, even from afar. Its iconic columns are lit up at night, and the slivered crescent moon hangs just above it. It might be the most beautiful thing I've ever seen.

Around the hill on which the Acropolis sits, Athens's nightlife bursts at the seams of the city. Chatter rises from the streets below, and I do my best to snatch at the words I know in the unfamiliar language. Our sleek rooftop patio is packed with people and the sounds of clinking drinks and cutlery. Our table is by the hedge outlining the edge of the roof, jasmine flowers bursting through the greenery. Their sweet scent freshens the air with the feeling of summer.

"This trip is going to blow my mind at every corner, huh?" I say. My eyes can't settle on any one thing. All of it—the streetlights casting a glow on the groups of people laughing their way down the street, the stray cats dashing across the road, the enduring remains of the ancient civilization watching over the whole scene—is too beautiful.

Liam is so enraptured by the view, he doesn't even hear me, but Melanie laughs.

"Yes," she says. "I haven't been many places, but all the same, I know Greece is the best place in the world."

I take a sip of the fruity mocktail I ordered, trying to ignore the way the moon seems to make Melanie's tanned skin glow. "Have you lived in Athens your whole life?"

She nods. "My mom teaches humanities at the American school here, so I've been going there since kindergarten. What about you?"

"I've been in New York my whole life," I tell her. "This is the first time I've left the city, actually."

She raises her eyebrows, smiling. "Wow. Welcome to somewhere else, then."

"Thanks," I laugh.

Liam finally manages to tear his eyes off the Acropolis to answer Melanie when she asks how we became friends. Our lore is one of my favorite stories. We both started at our middle school in seventh grade, two awkward new kids wondering how to make friends when everyone else had already settled into their middle school friend groups the year before.

And then we both failed our first math quiz so colossally that I started crying in the middle of the test period. He found me after class to tell me that he wanted to cry too, and when we found out we'd both gotten literally every single question wrong, our fate as best friends was sealed. Learning that he was also an ancient-world nerd on top of that just made it too good to be true.

Melanie laughs as Liam performs a reenactment of my math drama.

"Number four was just . . . so . . . impossible," he chokes out between fake sobs, and she snorts with laughter. Her eyes light up as she does, her smile transforming her whole face with its warm glow.

You can't actually like her, my brain reminds me. *She'd just see all the bad parts of you and run away. And maybe then Liam would see all the bad parts you've been hiding from him this whole time, and you'll lose him too. And then what will there be?*

I drown my thoughts with another sip of my drink. I don't need the reminder. There's no way I'm nursing a crush on Melanie. I'm just here to be her friend. Anything more would mean risking everything—and for what? A summer fling? A date to Lucy's precious end-of-trip party?

"Y'all are so cute," Melanie says.

"We're not a couple," I say quickly. Not that Melanie, specifically, needs to know that. It's just that nothing grinds my gears more than people assuming that Liam and I must be dating. Somehow, in the year of our Lord 2026, people are still wondering if men and women can really be friends. Even if everyone involved is literally gay.

"Duh," Melanie says. Her eyes meet mine, and for the briefest moment, I let myself melt into the warmth of her brown irises. It feels like she's seeing straight into me, and she wants to keep looking. Like she feels this too.

I blink at the thought and force myself to straighten my spine, moving away from her. Feeling *what* too? There's nothing here to feel.

"Sorry," Melanie says. "I shouldn't assume . . ."

"No, we're both quite gay," Liam says with a grin. "It makes the dating rumors even more exciting."

Melanie snorts. "Who the hell thinks you guys are dating?"

"Our teachers, half our classmates, most of my extended family, anyone who passes us on the street . . ." Liam counts on his fingers.

"It's the default assumption," I tell her, rolling my eyes. "It's this *thing* we always have to explain, and whether or not people believe us is sort of a coin toss. Half of everyone we know thinks we're at the beginning of a friends-to-lovers rom-com and just don't know it yet."

Melanie shakes her head. "That's so stupid."

It's a thought loop I've gotten caught in too often. So many people think I must be harboring secret romantic feelings for Liam. I've proven to myself—over and over and over again—that all the love I have for him is deeply platonic.

Still, I'm afraid to talk to Paige about that one. What if she says the thought loop is worth paying attention to?

"Well, I'm a lesbian too," Melanie says. "I get how endlessly frustrating that must be."

At the confirmation, my brain does a cute little short circuit. She's gay. So it's entirely possible she *does* feel it too. The way my face splotches red every time I look at her, the way looking into her eyes feels like looking at a work of art—could that be happening for her as well?

I mentally shake myself. I can't let my romantic nature win out over the part of me that knows I could never be in a relationship.

Melanie grins at me, and it lights up her whole face. "So, are either of you actually dating anyone?"

"Nope," Liam says before I can answer. "We're both single."

I fake a laugh and wrap my hands around his arm. "How dare you besmirch our relationship like that?"

Melanie snort-laughs. It's the cutest sound in the world.

I force myself to draw a breath in. It's not cute. Or, at least, not especially cute. It's just a laugh. All laughing is cute.

My head is spinning, and the thoughts are coming on too fast for me to process them. I can't fend off the thoughts about Melanie. Nor can I allow them in.

"Excuse me." I barely manage to choke out the words before I claw my way out of the booth and stumble to the bathroom. Mercifully, it's a single-stall situation. I lock the door behind me and sink to the floor, propping myself up on my heels.

You're always such a mess. It's exhausting.

The thought comes fast and rings in my ears like a slap. The thoughts keep coming, raining down on the coils of my brain, where there's nowhere I can escape.

If you fell in love with her, you'd have to let her in close enough to see this part of you.

The part that leaves me breathless on a bathroom floor, the cold of the tiles seeping through the thin material of my dress. Red blotching my pale cheeks, sweat tingeing the edges of my hair, fingers scrabbling at the grout.

If she saw this part of you, she'd never want you.

She'd tell the others.

It's a part of me I don't even let Liam see. I love him too much to let him know me like this. How could I possibly explain it? The way my thoughts can completely take over my body, the brain gremlin piloting my mind in directions that spin so far out of control, there seems to be nothing I can do to call it back.

So you have to keep her far away.

Paige always tells me to use my senses to come out of moments like this. I take a deep breath and notice what I smell. Wouldn't you know, it smells like bathroom in here. Great therapisting, Paige.

Although, the snarky thoughts about my therapist alert me to the fact that my brain has slowed. This thought spiral has set me free. For now.

Taking a shaky breath, I straighten my stiff legs and move to wash my hands. My reflection in the mirror above the sink captures all the panic that's been coursing through my veins. I let the cold water run a little too long over my hands, let it soothe my fingers, until the color of my cheeks returns to its usual pale tone.

I swing through the door and head back to our booth, where my two platonic besties await with piles of baklava warming the air between us.

Where I force laughter that sears when it comes up my throat, keeping everything they say at arm's length like a fire that might scald me if I get too close. Where I bite into the baklava every time I need to swallow down the urge to make a joke just to hear Melanie laugh.

Where I avoid direct contact with the warmth of her eyes for the rest of the night.

Summer Decathlon
Scavenger Hunt Items

1. A stray cat
2. An olive branch
3. The twelve gods and goddesses
4. Octopi drying on a line
5. An intact seashell
6. A dolphin
7. A philosopher
8. The collision of the ancient and modern worlds
9. Thought-provoking street art
10. A cheesy souvenir
11. A Greek flag
12. A fragment of ancient pottery
13. A lyra
14. Komboloi

CHAPTER THREE

WHEN I WAS IN SIXTH GRADE, my teacher taught us to annotate our books by looking for what he termed *signposts* in the text. One of them was called *again and again*. See something come up over and over again? Underline it with your green pen.

All this to say, being sweaty already by nine-thirty in the morning has green pen all over it.

Liam and I lean against each other as Ms. Barlowe herds us over to a waiting area so that she and Ms. Galanis can collect our group passes from the Acropolis ticketing booth. The leaning isn't out of affection but sheer necessity. If he weren't there to prop me up, I'd fall over from exhaustion. It's a bright two-thirty a.m. in New York right now, and I understand why Ms. Barlowe is obsessed with melatonin. My eye bags are digging canals across my face.

Melanie slumps over to us. She's clutching an iced coffee as big as her head (curls included). She makes eye contact with me as she takes a long sip. "I had fun last night, but right now I'm sort of regretting running into you people at the elevator."

"I'd say I'm sorry," I say, shrugging, "but I'm deeply not."

Melanie touches her fingers to her chest in mock tenderness. "That glad to spend the night with me?"

"More that my morning misery loves the company," I say with a grin.

She laughs, and I fight off with a spiked chain the thought that she has the cutest laugh ever. Paige says that OCD can come with intrusive thoughts, aka upsettingly unwanted thoughts my brain allegedly has a hard time fending off. That must be what this is.

Probably.

Before I can investigate this theory further, Ms. Barlowe and Ms. Galanis return with our tickets.

"Who's ready to see the Acropolis?"

Despite my exhaustion, I join in with the cheers that erupt from the rest of the group. I mean, it's the *Acropolis*. We all saw it from afar on our drive through Athens yesterday (and of course on our sneaky terrace trip), but now we're about to see it up close. Athena ranks high on everyone's list of favorite goddesses, and her most iconic temple is here.

Next to me, Lucy is practically vibrating. She's doing a chunk of her project on the Parthenon Marbles, and she's been talking nonstop about seeing the Acropolis in person. It might even outrank the food.

To get to the Parthenon, we hike up a marble-paved pathway that's already crowded with a thick line of tourists, even though we got here pretty early. I wait in line with my head on Liam's shoulder, taking in the views of the city as we make our way to the top of the rocky hill. The higher we climb, the more we can see of Athens unfurling below us. The Acropolis is surrounded by a large patch of greenery—tall, thin trees shooting straight up at us from below. Beyond them, the city sprawls outward, a collection of white buildings crowded together around the array of streets cutting through them.

We keep making our way up the sloped pathway to the Acropolis, the crowded line shuffling forward. The walkway is made slippery by the white marble paved over it, worn from the years of tourists forming the same line. Eventually, we reach the top. The slope flattens into a wide, rocky space that houses the ancient temple. As soon as we're past the entrance framed with columns on both sides, Lucy loops her arm around mine and pulls me straight for the Erechtheion, the smaller temple on the north side of the Acropolis. Because of course she does.

"Are you ready to see the caryatids?" she asks, referring to the statues of women who serve as the temple's columns.

"These are the copies," I remind her, and she shoots me a look that screams *Duh*.

"It's still *the* Erechtheion," she says, pulling up short when we reach it.

Even though I feel slightly silly standing with my back to the Parthenon, it's hard to deny the beauty of the smaller temple tucked in a corner of the wide-open space at the top of the hill. It's held up in part by the replicas of the six caryatids.

Five of the originals now live in the Acropolis Museum down the road, which opened in 2009 in an attempt to convince Britain to return all the Parthenon Marbles they stole. They did no such thing, because of course, and so the sixth caryatid still stands alone in the British Museum.

I know it's that thought that has Lucy choked up right now.

"They have to give her back."

"All of it," I agree.

The caryatid is the most famous of the missing marbles, but the British Museum is also holding on to 247 feet of the original Parthenon frieze—the intricate marble sculpture that decorated the upper part of the temple. It depicts a Panathenaic festival, in which Athens celebrated the birthday of their patron goddess, Athena.

The whole temple is dedicated to her, after one of my favorite stories. Poseidon and Athena once fought for the right to make the city theirs. In their contest, they offered the people two gifts. Poseidon's water spring was a massive disappointment, because the sea god made salt water run from the ground. Athena planted an olive tree, and with its high-quality wood and fruit that would make Greece's signature oil, it was the easy choice. The city became hers.

Like everyone else in the cohort, I'm not immune to fangirling over Athena. She's the goddess of wisdom, among other things, and that makes her an automatic headliner for a group of certified nerds like us. Knowing that these stones were erected in her honor over two thousand years ago and continue to watch over the city that still bears her name is enough to make me emotional.

Still arm in arm, Lucy and I turn to make our way around the Parthenon itself. The weight of her arm against mine is a bittersweet feeling. Lucy and I used to be on the path to becoming much closer friends. But then she caught me crying in the bathroom at school when I was freaking out about Amanda Goldstein asking me to homecoming. I made the mistake of trusting Lucy with the whole story—how I'd let myself flirt with Amanda for weeks while we struggled through our algebra problem sets, how her smile gave me butterflies, how it all became too real the second the question came out of her mouth and panic overtook me. How I'd found myself in the bathroom, overwhelmed with embarrassment at having led her on for so long, indulging my own wants, only to lose myself in the maze of my own fear at the thought of actually going out with her.

It was the moment when, caught crying in the bathroom with the heat of the emotions still coursing through me, I'd let my heart spill to Lucy.

"How are you supposed to know if someone is right for you?" I'd asked her, water running in the sink between us as she encouraged me to dab its coolness on my cheeks. "That they won't hurt you?"

It was that thought that had sent me running from my

algebra classroom. I hadn't started seeing Paige yet. Didn't know that I was so fundamentally wrecked, there was no way I could ever let someone truly get to know me deeply enough to love me like that.

"I don't think you can," Lucy had responded. She'd said more, about things being worth the risk, but I'd taken it as all the confirmation I needed. No amount of fun at homecoming was worth the risk of ending up hurt because I went with the wrong person.

After that I was too embarrassed to look Lucy in the face, let alone hang out with her anymore. Every time I saw her, the shame of that moment, of having spilled so much of myself, came rushing back.

We never had a fight, but the closeness of our friendship petered out, a skipping stone that sunk to the sandy depths before it could make it out to sea. I wish I could call it back to the surface, retrace its original path, but I'm not sure how to do that without acknowledging what happened. And *that* I definitely don't know how to do.

"I want to incorporate the frieze into my project some-how," Lucy tells me now. "Maybe some kind of contemporary element to translate it culturally."

"You could recast the people on it as modern figures," I suggest. A voice in the back of my head whispers that I should keep my mouth shut, that I'm just helping the competition.

But then Lucy brightens, and I drop the thought. That can't be the vibe of this trip. And that's no way to resuscitate our friendship.

As we make our way to the far end of the Parthenon, pausing to admire the ancient white stones towering above us, we giggle as we come up with increasingly ridiculous ideas for who Lucy should add to her contemporary frieze.

"I'm putting the cast of *Mamma Mia!* on horseback," Lucy says, and I collapse into laughter against her shoulder.

We're both laughing so hard that we don't notice Melanie walking toward us until I bump into her. She's still nursing her massive frappé, although an alarming amount of it is gone, considering it's only been half an hour since I saw it full.

"Want some?" She holds it out to me, grinning. "I see that exhausted, yearning stare."

I laugh again. "You're my savior."

"Once again," Melanie teases.

I take a long sip. It's stronger than I expected, though to be fair, my usual order is a chai latte that's more syrup than caffeine. The coffee flavor jolts through me, a burst of energy that I desperately needed.

"Thanks," I say as I hand it back to her. "That did indeed save me."

"Happy to help." Melanie squints as the sun hits her eyes, transforming them into a pool of amber. I could drown in them.

I blink the thought away. Intrusive. Probably brought on by caffeine overdose.

As soon as Melanie is out of earshot, Lucy turns to me with the kind of grin that makes my blood run cold, even though the rising temperatures and hike up to the top of the Acropolis have made me sweatier still.

"What?" I ask, folding my arms. A soft summer breeze rustles past us, stirring the dust layered over the rocky surface of the plateau. I let the gentleness of the air wrap around my skin, soothing me enough that I dare meet Lucy's gaze.

"Melanie's cute, huh?"

I take an interest in the Doric columns that make up the Parthenon's peristyle. The timeworn white marble towers over us. The wind whistles through the empty spaces between them, dust swirling up to the open space above, where the roof once sat. "Do you want to comment on the British Museum controversy in your project?"

"Duh," Lucy says. "Not an interesting-enough subject change. Do you like her?"

I wince. Even before I broke down in the bathroom in front of Lucy, I was never super into crush culture. The way people's real feelings get turned into sleepover entertainment, the teachers who make jokes on social media about playing matchmaker with their seating charts, the entitlement people feel to pester one another about *who they like*. It's always struck me as kind of weird. The last thing I want right now is to be interrogated about my (*very platonic*) feelings for Melanie, for them to be twisted into something more so that Lucy can have her fun.

But this take has gotten me in hot water before, namely when I almost had to out myself in a seventh-grade game of truth-or-dare because no one would let it go when I didn't want to talk about my crush. As if that should automatically be public information.

"She seems really cool," I say in a measured voice. "I'd like to be her friend."

Lucy sighs. "I don't mean to put you on the spot. I get that it's scary. I just think you could let yourself live a little."

I want to seize this opening and run with it. I want to tell her how sorry I am for letting our friendship fall by the wayside. But the thought of actually saying that out loud feels akin to picking up a beehive and smashing it on the ground. A bee swarm attack sounds preferable to unleashing the sting of a conversation about my feelings.

Besides, I don't agree with her. I live just fine. I don't need to risk my heart on a summertime fling when there's no way to know if she's the right person for me or how things would turn out. If it'd be fun or if I'd go home irreparably damaged by the weeds of a toxic romance.

I've heard enough of Lizzie's high school dating stories to know that things can go badly. I'm not risking that.

Worse yet, I could get outed as a certifiable loser who can't even get through a meal with a potential crush without spiraling on the bathroom floor. I don't need anyone—not Melanie, not anyone she might tell if she ever got close enough to me to find out—to know about that.

So I settle for shrugging.

"Just don't shut yourself down reactionarily," Lucy says in response. "You deserve better from yourself than that. You deserve to be open to the world."

None of that makes sense to me. What if I think Melanie could be the one for me, but it turns out I'm making a huge mistake? But arguing about it with Lucy is a path that leads straight to verbal quicksand. So I nod politely, like I do when my mom starts lecturing me about how math is more important than the classics and I should spend as much time on algebra as I do on the myths. As if.

"You're probably right," I say.

She beams. "So I can help with Melanie?"

"I wouldn't go that far."

She gives me a withering look, and I gesture at the literal Parthenon right in front of us. "Isn't there enough going on this summer?"

"Trying to limit the pleasures life has to offer?" Lucy squeezes my arm. "That is not a vibe the ancient Greeks would have approved of."

I shake my head as I let her lead me the rest of the way around the temple. I'll let her say whatever she wants, but when it comes to putting myself out there, I have no intention of listening.

Liam has somehow written two pages' worth of poetry in his notebook by the Parthenon. I left him unattended for ten seconds, and he spat out a masterpiece. Even though I barely drifted away from Lucy's side, her notebook is full of scribbled ideas. Amalia walks down the tree-lined road to the Acropolis Museum with a stack of notebooks in her arms, the top one open to the middle so she can add more writing.

I brought my study materials for the day, of course, but my

notebook has yet to leave my tote. The bag slaps against my side as I walk, reminding me with every bounce against my hip of how behind I'm falling. I don't get how they can all do this so easily. Just put aside whatever's worrying them for the day and focus on what's in front of them. My view of the space in front of me is always marred by the thoughts that spill over from my constantly whirring brain.

I tried explaining it to Paige once, but I don't think she got what I meant. It barely makes sense to me, so I can't blame her for not getting it. Just further proof that I'm quite unfixable.

We're making our way down the paved path from the Acropolis to its accompanying museum. The path is lined with greenery, livening the air with the sweet smell of summer leaves. I'm grateful for the trees, which cast sun-dappled shadows along the walkway, rescuing us from the beating rays of the midday sun.

It all feels like the Platonic ideal of a summer day. The sun illuminates a crisp blue sky, wrapped around the greenery of the earth. Even the sweat slipping down my neck feels sweet, cooling me with every breeze that rustles past the leaves to us.

"We're going to have a couple of hours in the museum," Ms. Barlowe says as we pass under a huge column to reach the glass front doors. Next to me, Lucy strains for her first look into the museum. Melanie, I notice with disappointment as I scan the group, has disappeared.

"We booked you audio tours, which Ms. Galanis is getting right now, and then we'll set you loose," Ms. Barlowe continues.

As soon as Lucy gets her hands on an audio guide, she disappears into the museum. I know she's making a beeline for the caryatids. Liam hauls his art supplies out of his canvas bag, ready to be one of those cool art students painting in a corner of a room. As I follow my cohort inside, I'm struck not for the first time by how impressive my classmates are. So many of them have already uncovered their niches as artists, as scholars, as writers. As someone who's armed only with a passion for Artemis, I'm intimidated as hell.

Liam always tries to remind me that I'm the only freshman in the program when what he calls *my imposter syndrome* kicks in. (*I* call it *my accurate self-assessment*, but he's not having that.) But he's only a sophomore and already writing some of the greatest mythology-inspired poetry I've ever read. So who is he to talk?

It's cool inside the museum, the sunlight filtering through the dark tinted windows, a relief from the already climbing outdoor temperature. I dab at the sweat lining my brow as I trail after Liam. We decide to start on the third floor, where the gallery is set up with the original Parthenon frieze. As soon as we get there, I'm floored by the beauty of the space. The frieze blocks are laid out along four inner walls to mirror their original positioning in the Parthenon, and statues from the Parthenon pediments are displayed in the wide-open space around the frieze. Through the glass walls, we have a perfect view of the Acropolis, the frieze blocks watching over their first home.

"It's beautiful," I breathe.

Liam nods. "It's actually hitting me today. That we're here."

The sheer age of everything we've seen today is overwhelming in and of itself. The Acropolis has been standing watch over this city for more than two thousand years. It was that long ago that skilled artists' hands carved into the marble blocks we stand among now, so many years later, to admire their handiwork and the stories they told.

Ancient history never fails to give me chills.

Liam wraps his arm around my shoulders, and I turn into him to return the hug. He doesn't have to say what he's thinking, because I know the same gratitude is running through my mind. I can't believe I'm lucky enough to be here, in this unbelievably special place, with my best friend.

"Let's find you some Artemis," he says with a grin.

As we make our way around the frieze, I try to add as much as I can to my notebook. It somehow isn't much. Every time I reach for my pen, my fingers freeze up, paralyzed by doubt. Everyone else in my program is *so good* at what they do. How can I ever hope to measure up?

It's enough to make me wonder if I should bother entering the decathlon at all or just admit defeat now. Give in to my parents and focus more on math, let my dream of the classics shrivel.

It's the kind of thing I wonder if I should talk to Paige about. She's huge on telling me that I can *always reach out if I need to talk, even from Greece!* But first of all, bothering her outside of our sessions feels akin to sending food back at a restaurant because they forgot I asked for no cheese. I'd sooner choke down the parmesan on my pasta than bother someone who's just trying to do their job.

Besides, she would just tell me to enter anyway. Face my fears! Woo-hoo! If it were that easy, I wouldn't need to talk to her in the first place.

We wander slowly through the rest of the museum, and I make Liam stop at a statue of the face of Artemis. I have no idea what I'm doing for my project yet, but I snap a million photos of the statue on my phone. I love photography, even if my only equipment is the camera app, and I do my best to capture the worn edges of the statue, the way it's been broken down over its long history. While I have my phone out, I also take a picture of the Acropolis framed by the modern metal framework outlining the window of the museum.

"Gorgeous," Liam says, leaning over my shoulder to watch me work. "You should do a photography project."

The idea occurred to me as soon as I found out we were coming to Greece, that I would be able to look directly at these ancient places and their artifacts myself—and point my camera at them. But Liam's an artistic genius, and Lucy is already incorporating a visual piece into her project. Next to them, anything I do will fall completely flat.

"Maybe," I tell Liam. "Could be cool. Thanks."

I hate the way my brain functions a lot of the time. My inner monologue is just nonstop whining. The last thing I want to do most of the time is speak any of it aloud. No one needs to hear my complaining.

Not even Paige!

Unfortunately, Liam knows me better than Paige does.

"What's up?" he asks as we make our way through the rows of marble statues, pausing to read every informational placard.

"I'm just nervous about the project," I admit. "The competition piece is getting in my head a little. Like, knowing I'll be judged against everyone else."

"I hate it," Liam says. I look up at him, surprised. Liam is on the soccer team and does Model UN. He's not exactly a stranger to competition or being judged against his opponents.

Seeing my expression, he shrugs. "We should be able to uplift each other's research and knowledge, not be pitted against each other. In this context, competition helps no one."

He's not wrong. I'm already feeling so worn down by the idea that we're all going to be judged not just on how well we do, but whether we do better than our peers, that any ability I had to think of an idea is totally fried.

It doesn't help that part of me can't stop wondering where Melanie went.

But I can't fix any of this now.

Instead, I try to throw myself into the museum as we keep touring. Everything we pass is a marvel, and I have to drag myself away from every statue and artifact to make it to the next one. It's the perfect, necessary reminder of why I'm here. I didn't come to Greece to rank myself against my friends or fend off crush accusations left and right. I'm here because my whole life is about studying the classics. I love the way these stories still feel so *alive*, even thousands of years after they were first told, and as I stand here among some of the most precious pieces of art they inspired, that's never felt more true.

I just need to put everything else to the side and focus on the love of art that brought me here in the first place.

The timing of this trip is impeccable. Never has there been a better excuse to get out of a summer full of wedding planning and college-dorm-room packing.

Until now.

"What do you think?" Lizzie asks. She's holding two swatches of blue fabrics up to her phone screen on FaceTime. I'm afraid to say they look absolutely identical because, based on the feral look in her eyes, I'm sure she'll go all Miranda Priestly monologue on me if I do.

"The one on the right," I say instead.

"My right or yours?"

"Uh. Yours."

She lifts one of the blue fabrics, and I nod, pulling the thin white blanket on my hotel bed up higher around my waist.

"This and then carrying white flowers?" Lizzie says.

It's possible that agreeing to be a bridesmaid was the worst choice I've ever made in my life. At least the color of the dress is pretty. A light blue in gauzy fabric to match her late-summer wedding vibes. Andrea and I will look adorable.

"It's perfect," I tell Lizzie. I've learned these are the only words that will turn off any given debate. If you ask me, she's the one who should be talking to Paige. But of course, my parents approve of romance-related periods of foolishness.

"Thanks." She sighs, flopping back onto the plush green armchair that sits in a corner of her living room. "This stuff is killing me. Did you know picking out napkins is a thing?"

"Can't you just bring some paper towels and call it a day?"

This is a joke, but joking near wedding planning has been classified as a life-threatening activity that should only be attempted by a stunt double. Lizzie rolls her eyes at me.

"Honestly, Natalie, this is going to be a nice event. I'm getting *married*. You only do that once."

Unless you get divorced is what I don't say. Not because I don't like Mason, her fiancé. He's fine. I mean, he's just some guy, but he's fine. It's the multithousand-dollar flower budget I object to more than anything else. That and the inherent performativity of the contemporary wedding industry, but if I bring that up at this point, I'll probably be excommunicated from my family.

So a baby blue bridesmaid's dress it is.

"How's everything else going?" I ask Lizzie.

She huffs, her eyebrows scrunching. "Work is an everlasting nightmare. And they have no sympathy for how stressful wedding planning is."

I resist the urge to groan. My sisters have always been many milestones ahead of me. With Andrea, who's only three years ahead of me, it's mostly fine, but Lizzie is a decade older than I am. When I was younger, she felt like a cool, aspirational, auntlike figure. Now that Andrea is leaving for college, it feels more like my entire family has grown up and moved on. And I'm still stuck in high school. For *three more years.*

"What else do you have to do?" I ask, instead of delving into any of that with Lizzie.

She explains the politics of seating arrangements, and to be fair, I don't envy her having to figure out how to seat our family, given Aunt Stacey and Aunt Pam's latest feud.

I just wish she'd also think to ask about my trip.

Chapter Four

HOTEL BREAKFASTS ARE ONE OF THE most underrated joys
this earth has to offer. I'm usually not one for early rising, but
the promise of tiny baked goods and slightly overcooked eggs
has me bouncing down the stairs by six-thirty a.m. in spite of
the jet lag.

I expected to be the first one to reach the breakfast room,
a small and brightly lit nook across from the front desk, but
someone's already there when I walk in.

Melanie.

She's pouring herself a massive cup of coffee, and she
wrinkles her nose when she takes a sip.

"This tastes like garbage," she says cheerfully when she
sees me. "I don't know why I agreed to stay at the hotel with
y'all. I could've had access to my own coffee maker the whole
time we're in Athens."

"But then what would you do for tiny pastries?" I ask, clicking the tongs at her before picking out a mini chocolate croissant and a little baklava that the hotel staff has generously put out even though this is, objectively speaking, not a breakfast food. I respect anyone who shares my worldview that anything can be a breakfast food so long as you believe.

"That and not commuting for an hour to join my mom on the outings," Melanie says, but she helps herself to a Breakfast Baklava™ all the same.

Our plates loaded up with an appropriate amount of breakfast food (read: half the buffet), we make our way to one of the smooth wood tables in the corner. I sit across from her, and Lucy's words ring in my ears: *Be open to the world.*

"Where did you disappear to yesterday?" I ask.

Melanie flexes an eyebrow. "Miss me?"

"Desperately," I say, the corners of my lips quirking up. Maybe being open means I can have a little flirt, as a treat. It doesn't have to mean anything. Flirting with friends is just a fun, friendly time!

"One of my friends was having a graduation party, so I went over there early to help her get set up," she says.

My shoulders slump. I'd thought Melanie was younger, like me. "You graduated this year?"

"No," Melanie says, her tone shockingly bitter. "Just all my friends. I . . ." She trails off for a moment, staring into the depths of her coffee. "I was a sophomore, but most of my friends this year were seniors. From drama club. There was . . . drama." She spins the coffee mug between her palms, her eyes still downcast, and I can tell there's more to the story. I know what it's like for people to come at your soul with pliers, though, so I don't ask her to share anything she hasn't volunteered already.

Instead, I nod sympathetically. "My sisters are both a billion years older than me. The middle one graduated a couple of weeks ago; the oldest is getting married at the end of the summer. I get what it's like to feel left behind."

"Yeah. And, like, what am I going to do next year?" Melanie says. She says it like she's telling a joke, but her voice carries the weight of thick emotion.

I reach across the table to squeeze her hand. Her skin is soft against mine, our fingers entwining easily, and she gives me a grateful smile.

And listen, I'm a "physical touch is my love language" kind of person. I've held hands with all my friends a million times. But it's never felt like *this*. Our eyes meet over our joined hands, and I catch my heart yearning. For what, I'm not sure. All I know is the weight of her hand feels natural in mine, like it belongs there.

Maybe it's simply because we were confiding in each other. Maybe the added weight of this moment just comes from the emotions we're both bringing to this little breakfast table. For a second, I feel caught in the moment, unsure whether—or how—to lean in or pull away from it.

If you lean in, she'll see you.

All of you.

And then she'll run away from you.

Friendship is better. Safer. It gives me room to enjoy our summer together, keeping her at arm's length until there's an ocean between us again.

The reminder is enough to make me pull back. I slip my fingers away from hers and back to my side of the table under the guise of taking another bite of baklava. It might as well be cardboard. I chew mechanically, forcing myself to swallow without gagging.

If she notices the spiral behind my eyes, Melanie doesn't say anything. She just gives me a small smile before taking another sip of her coffee. She doesn't bother hiding her gag.

"Really, that's disgusting," she says. "Who is responsible for this garbage?"

I laugh. "We need to get you another frappé."

"Immediately," Melanie says with a nod. She scoots her chair back from the table a bit. "Want to come with? There's a place around the corner that's solid."

I'm ready to say yes. Keep talking as I walk with her around the corner, get a frappé myself, and spend the day giggling together about how jittery and overly caffeinated I am. It sounds nice. Natural, even.

But I know where that leads. An easy, smooth beginning that slides fast into a disastrous chaos of balancing on a tightrope that only grows thinner. There's no way I'd be able to keep my balance.

Instead, I gesture to my pajamas. "I should probably get ready for the day."

"Oh." Melanie looks surprised for a moment, and I shrink

under the realization that she expected me to say yes. To be excited to go with her. The same way Amanda Goldstein reacted when I gave her such a hard no to homecoming. She tried to hide it, but I could tell that she was hurt for weeks afterward, and we never found our way back to complaining about algebra in quite the same lighthearted tone. I'm pretty sure her best friend still hates me for it. Worse still, I can't say I blame her.

Guilt blossoms in my chest, its tendrils wrapping around my lungs.

The small part of me that yearned to hold her hand longer kindles again. Ease the disappointment, take back the way I've made her feel.

I stamp out the sparks before they can turn into a flame.

"No worries," Melanie says, quickly smoothing over the little awkwardness. "See you for the tour?"

"Of course," I say with a smile. "Next time for the coffee?"

I don't know why it slips out, but her eyes light up when I say it, so I'm glad I did.

"Next time," she agrees.

We part ways at the lobby, her heading out and me lingering like a fool before making my way back to the elevator. I slam my fingers into the button for my floor, and it feels like admitting defeat.

If I'm sacrificing everything to focus on this stupid project, I should probably focus on it. That's what I tell myself as we bustle off the metro and out into the busy streets of Monasti-raki. It's a flea-market neighborhood surrounded by several important ancient sites, and as soon as we're aboveground, I'm greeted by an explosion of color. The stands crowd against each other on both sides of every street, bursting with woven bags made of overlapping colors, fancy glass bottles of olive oil, and linen dresses flapping in the breeze. The smoke rising from the food vendors' stands mix in the middle of the street, the smell of crisping meat for Lucy's next gyro washing over us. Even the streets themselves, a bright array of small cob-blestoned tiles, add to the color of the neighborhood.

The metro exit let us out onto a wide plaza, which breaks off into smaller streets that narrow as they wind upward. Crowds of people hustle past us as our group gets its bear-ings, gathering around Ms. Barlowe in a corner of the main square. Here we're mostly surrounded by modern apartment buildings, balconies covered in greenery, and local chain res-taurants advertising their lunch offerings in loud lettering.

But amid all the chaos of life in the city center juts out the Church of Panagia Pantanassa. It's an ancient structure that's been standing here, watching its surroundings change, since the tenth century. It is small and unassuming amid the busy-ness of the square, its ancient stone walls and worn red-tiled roof seemingly stuck out of place and time.

I break away from the group for a quick second to frame the perfect photo, capturing both the church and the bright neon sign of the sandwich place behind it. The picture joins my camera roll next to a photo I just took of the ruins, discovered by accident when the train tunnels were dug, heaped up in the Monastiraki metro station.

"The whole neighborhood is named for it," Ms. Barlowe is saying when I return. "It's the *little monastery*, and in Greek, *aki* is a diminutive suffix. Hence, Monastiraki."

We're starting the day with a tour of the ancient Roman Forum and shopping around the flea market before spending the afternoon at the National Archaeological Museum and Museum of Cycladic Art. I can't wait for any of it. The perfect day to completely immerse myself in the ancient world, in learning, in work on my project. And ignore everything else.

Like the way Melanie's laughter fills the street.

I fight the urge to turn and stare jealously at whoever made her laugh. Instead, I force myself to pay attention as Ms. Galanis explains the history of the neighborhood. None of her words seem to make it through my ears, and the array of colors and spiced smells and overlapping vendor voices from the flea market turn into a dull blur around me. All I can process is the rush of inescapable thinking. Everything I said and thought and decided this morning at breakfast with Melanie on loop. A merry-go-round from hell. Wheeeeeee.

We make our way up one of the side streets, crowded on both sides by tourists pushing their way to the market stalls lining the sidewalks. Ms. Barlowe keeps talking about the agora we're headed to see, but the voices of the vendors and shoppers around us drown out her explanation. It's hard to imagine that anything could fit in this neighborhood other than the goods for sale.

In fact, it's hard to believe this amount of wares has managed to fit on a single street.

But then, as if to prove me wrong, Hadrian's Library comes into view on our left. Protected by a wrought iron fence, the remains of its ancient Roman architecture stand opposite a closed, graffitied storefront and a series of flea-market dress vendors, their blue and white linens hanging off lines strung across the outer walls of their stalls.

Liam nudges my shoulder, but I ignore him when I realize that his eyes are trained on Melaine. The last thing I need is to spend more time leading her on after our disastrous breakfast this morning.

Instead, I take more photos of the juxtaposition as we keep walking past, the lines of market stalls transforming into tavernas as we round the corner to the next street. A handful of early lunchers sit in the shade of wide-open umbrella stands, fanning themselves with touristy paneled maps of the area. Before I know it, we're in front of the Roman Forum. Liam and Bodhi crowd next to me as we bunch up around the fence to get a better look at the ruins. Even in ruins, the columns are impressive. Most of the forum is gone, a few quarter columns from the original peristyle remaining in lines along the sides of the space, but the entryway is still largely intact. It's a huge gate supported by four Doric columns, standing watch over the little patches of greenery that lay beyond. I take more photos, even though at this point, I've more than fulfilled the scavenger hunt's demands for photos of the ancient and modern worlds clashing. But I feel the need to do something to occupy my hands, as everyone around me is busy with their projects.

Amalia has her notebook out and is scribbling so fast, the tip of her mechanical pencil breaks multiple times against the page. George glances over at her notes, and she shoots him a look before shifting the cover to shield her writing. He rolls his eyes.

"What are you even doing for your project?" he asks.

"Not telling," Amalia says.

"Calm down. I'm not going to steal your idea," George says.

Amalia fixes him with a glare so fierce, I'm scared to look straight at it. "Like how you weren't going to use my artwork in your project last year?"

"That was inspiration," George whines. "I didn't literally use your artwork."

"Whatever." Amalia turns back to her notes, writing at double speed to catch up on the precious seconds she wasted indulging George.

Liam and I exchange looks. I was still in middle school last year, so I'm not as familiar with this particular drama, but Liam gave me daily updates as it unfolded. As low-key as a plagiarism scandal can be, it still lit up the whole cohort for a solid month as everyone debated whether George's cover artwork infringed too much on the sketches he'd borrowed from Amalia.

I thought they'd moved past it by now. Amalia's quick

temper burns like a sudden flame—hot, bright, and of short duration. For the year I've known them, they've been famous friends. But now the tension between them prickles in the air around us all.

"I hope something new didn't happen," Liam whispers to me as we walk around the fencing, Ms. Galanis explaining more about the forum as we go.

"Same," I mutter. I create enough drama all by myself in my own head without the cohort exploding again.

We tour the agora, and I find myself wishing that some of the columns were still standing at their full height so that I could get some shade. The sun is doing some serious beaming, and I'm slick with sweat in what I'm sure is an extremely unattractive fashion.

Not that I care about being attractive, necessarily. But Melanie somehow looks amazing. Not even a hair out of place. It's borderline rude.

An hour later, Ms. Barlowe releases us for lunch and shopping around Monastiraki before we head off for our afternoon of museuming.

I expect us all to stay together, the way we did in Syntagma on our first day. But Amalia drifts away from George, pairing off with Henry. George and Bodhi are already halfway down the street. Lucy finds Liam and me, her eyes bright.

"Want to join me on my quest for pastitsio?" she asks. It's a lasagna-like Greek dish she had for dinner last night and immediately declared her new one true love.

"It would be our honor," Liam says. He takes cravings seriously, one of the many things I love about him.

I think, for a moment, about inviting Melanie to join us, but she's deep in conversation with her mom. Besides, I'm still freaked from our conversation this morning. If I don't watch my thoughts closely enough, they drift back to the feeling of her hand in mine, a memory that lights up my gut with anxious fluttering.

I can't keep putting myself through it.

In any case, Lucy and Liam are already making their way down the street, heading back through the flea market on their way to lunch. I fall into step beside them, and this time I force myself to pay attention. The vendors are selling everything from floaty Grecian dresses to blue evil-eye jewelry. My meager savings from my after-school job folding clothes and being yelled at by customers at a clothing store fall in deep danger whenever we pass a fancy-looking bottle of olive oil.

"So, what's up with Amalia and George?" Lucy asks as we stop to examine a spinning rack of postcards. "Because I can't handle another group drama."

"They have their shit," Liam says with a shrug. "We don't have to all get involved again. That was the mistake last time."

Lucy nods but looks unconvinced. "I'm definitely not picking sides again."

From what I remember of Liam's story, she was on Team Amalia last year but was also the first to forgive George when he apologized.

"I'm just nervous, I guess," Lucy says. "I wanted us to come together on this trip. Really have a bonding thing."

Lucy's one of the recently graduated seniors, so it's easy to see where she's coming from. This trip is her last time being part of this cohort.

Liam nods. "I'm sure it'll be okay."

But as we make our way toward pastitsio, I think about how quickly the group splintered off, and I realize I don't share his certainty.

We've only been full-time tourists for a couple of days, but all the uphill walking through Monastiraki and standing in the cool, dark rooms of the Museum of Cycladic Art burn in my calves. As soon as we get back to the hotel, I flop back onto the bed, propping my sore feet on top of the headboard. Liam invited me to join him on an outing to explore the neighborhood surrounding our hotel, but our abstracts, signifying our formal entries into the decathlon, are due tonight, and I still have no idea what I want to do for my project. My evening is bookmarked for academia.

Now that I'm alone in the hotel room with nothing but a blank notebook page to keep me company, I lightly regret my decision. I have to come up with something impressive enough to explain my presence in this program, and I only have a handful of hours to do it.

I click my pen again, hoping this will spark some kind of inspiration. My backup idea about the followers of Artemis feels so dull compared to what everyone else in the cohort is doing. I'll fall completely flat on my face if that's what I submit.

My brainstorming, if you can call it that, is interrupted by a knock at the door. I roll my eyes as I swing my legs around and hop off the bed, ready to tease Liam about already having lost his hotel room key.

But the joke dies against my teeth when the door opens to reveal Melanie, standing in the hallway in an all-pink pajama getup, holding a plate of baklava.

"Liam told me you were staying behind to work," she says, lifting the plate. "I figured you could use some sustenance to help you out."

I smile in spite of myself as I take in the embroidered floral detailing on her pajama tank top and baggy shorts. The last thing I should do is let myself stew in this feeling, but I find myself holding the door open wider to invite her in.

I mean, she brought me dessert. Surely it would be rude not to.

Grinning in a way that makes me feel like I must have made the right choice, Melanie slips past me into the room. We settle, cross-legged, on opposite sides of the bed, the plate of baklava and two forks between us.

"I hope I didn't ruin your plans for the night," I say softly. I knot my fingers in my lap, unsure of what to do with myself. If I were to give in to what I *want* to do, my hands would be around Melanie's by now, indulging again in the softness of her skin against mine.

But then I'd just be falling into my same pattern. Opening a door I have no intention of walking through.

It's just safer to keep it closed tight.

"Of course not," Melanie says with an easy laugh. I let myself relax into its sound. *There's no reason to be nervous*, I tell myself. *I'm just hanging out with a friend, having dessert and complaining about school. It's nothing I haven't done a million times over. No reason why this should be different from any other night.*

"If anything, you're saving me," she adds.

"Oh? What from?"

"My mom nagging me to join the competition," Melanie says with an eye roll. "She refuses to grasp that her love of the humanities is just not a gene she passed down to me."

She juts her chin toward one of the forks, and I pick it up to dig into the baklava. The crispy upper layer sprays a dash of crumbs on the bedspread as I slice the baklava in half. The honeyed pistachio layers melt against my tongue, and I have to suppress a groan.

Melanie does no such thing when she takes her first bite. "Okay, their coffee is a flop, but this hotel knows what they're doing with the desserts."

"It's no breakfast baklava," I say with a teasing grin, "but it'll do."

As soon as the words are out of my mouth, I regret them. She mirrors my smile, and on her face, I see how flirty it seems on top of my completely unnecessary reference to our cozy morning in a little corner of the breakfast nook.

I try to bury the light, tugging feeling in my chest with another bite of baklava, crispy crumbs sticking to my lips. The feeling is still there, tight against my heart, pulling me toward her.

"I think you have me ready to convert to breakfast-dessert personhood," Melanie admits.

"It's the best," I assure her. "Why start the day by depriving yourself of the best things life has to offer?"

"It's a point I simply can't argue with."

I laugh, the tension in my shoulders dissolving. It's easy, being here with Melanie. She makes me feel light enough to forget that I was supposed to be worrying about something.

It's not a relief I experience often, and I let myself exhale into it.

"So, how's the work going?" Melanie asks. It should be enough to bring the panic right back, but that calm smile lingers on her face, spreading its peace into my chest.

"It's quite tragic, I fear," I tell her, nodding to my all-too-blank notebook. "As you can see, I am not drowning in a wealth of ideas."

"Neither would I be, in your shoes," Melanie assures me.

"I think the key difference here is that I *am* a classics person," I remind her.

She leans to rest on her side, propping herself up with her elbow. The duvet folds around her, hugging her back, and I'm filled with the sudden wild thought that I wish I could hold her that close. Let her be that close to me.

But of course, the thought is enough to send all my spiked

defenses on full alert. I fold my legs against my chest instead, resting my chin on my knees.

"That was your first mistake," Melanie says with another teasing smile. She reaches over to pat my leg, and my skin flames at her touch. "It's not too late to change course."

The heat of her hand is enough to coax me out of my protective shell. I stretch out my legs in front of me, my hands curling around my knees. She slides her hand to meet mine, and before I can so much as draw a breath, I'm holding on to her, our fingers entwined.

"Changing course sounds nice right about now," I admit. Her thumb runs slow, lazy circles against the back of my hand, at once calming my muscles and egging on the thought spiral that seems to follow her movements.

How can something that feels this right end up being wrong?

But doesn't it always feel right in the beginning? How can you ever really know if it is?

Best to run away. It's always best to run away. But I find myself sitting up, reaching for my laptop.

"Maybe I just need to take a break," I hear myself say. "Wanna watch *Mamma Mia!*?"

I watched the sequel on the plane, and the soundtrack has been blasting in my headphones ever since. An hour and forty-eight minutes of silliness set to ABBA sounds like exactly what I need right now.

And if Melanie has to sit close enough to me for us to share the view of my laptop screen, so be it.

She shifts on the bedspread to settle next to me, our shoulders touching, our hands still linked between our thighs. As I start the movie, I'm hyperaware of every cell in my body, every inhale I take, every beat of my heart. *Mamma Mia!* is one of my favorite movies, but I barely notice it go by in front of me. I'm too focused on the heat of Melanie's hand, the swirl of Melanie's thumb pushing against my skin, asking with every swish: *What are you doing?*

The Fam

LIZZIE: I'm just saying that not even all of YOU have rsvp'ed

ANDREA: I've been BUSYYYYY

LIZZIE: Busy driving me nuts

LIZZIE: <3

MOM: And Natalie is in Greece! Natalie, have you been keeping up with Paige while you've been gone?

DAD: Natalie, answer your mother!

CHAPTER FIVE

THE THING ABOUT BUS RIDES WITH students is that they are loud. I mean, there are only eight of us on this bus, and I'm staring in despondent silence out the window, but somehow the volume of our overlapping voices strains against the walls. I don't let that get in the way of my despondency, though. Nothing could stop me from being maudlin today.

So I'm sitting by myself at the front of the bus, having claimed nausea to beg off joining Melanie and the rest of the cohort where they've set up camp, and I'm taking in the views of Greece flashing by. We're driving just over an hour to Sounion and the ruins of the Temple of Poseidon. So far the drive has been breathtaking, and I'm trying to let the natural beauty of Greece take me away from the relentlessness of my thoughts.

I mostly fail at this, but the trying feels worth it.

My thoughts are finally interrupted by the shifting in my seat. I turn to see Melanie settling next to me, smiling. "Cool if I join you?"

I nod, because what else am I supposed to say?

"Thanks," she says. "The car sickness caught up to me too."

"Yeah, it's tough," I say, turning back to the window. "Watching the horizon helps."

We sit in silence for a while, and to my surprise, it doesn't feel awkward. Having her next to me feels natural, companionable, even though we're not saying anything.

I do my best to stamp out the feeling. I've already done more than enough damage after last night. What was I thinking, letting myself hold her hand like that? Ignoring my abstract just to watch a movie I've already seen a billion times with a girl I vowed to stay far away from?

I ended up submitting a half-hearted proposal with no specifics about how I'd present my findings on Artemis or her followers. I have basically nothing to offer the program, and now the fancy fellowship people can see that in clear black-and-white print. All because I let feelings be more important than what I said mattered most to me.

Her smile this morning, if I let myself look at it for too long, makes me feel like it might have been worth it.

I look away. Nothing can be worth giving up myself. Not even if it feels right in the moment.

After last night, I feel like I'm trapped at the bottom of a well with no clue how to claw myself back out.

I even tried going for a run this morning. I wasn't going

to make myself commit to keeping up with my track training during the trip, what with how unbearably hot it is here and all the work I'm supposed to be doing on the project, but I thought running might help me clear my head. My heart rate just kept up with the pounding of my feet against the pavement, each beat shouting about Melanie.

"Did you enjoy breakfast as much this morning?" Melanie asks.

I blink and turn back to her. "Oh. Yeah. Breakfast baklava always hits."

"I'm coming around to your worldview," Melanie says.

"What about the coffee?"

She wrinkles her nose. "That I will never come around to. And I overslept this morning, so I didn't have time to get a frappé."

"Your life is a tragedy," I groan. "No one deserves a day of no frappé."

"That rhymed," Melanie says with a delighted smile. "Which almost makes up for it. Plus I got one after lunch."

"Glad I could help." I meet her eye—always a huge mistake. It's so easy to lose myself in the flecks of gold as the sun hits her brown irises. I can see her smile reaching to her eyes, and it's impossible not to return it.

But then her fingers inch toward mine. It's a small movement, but it's enough to put a tiny crack in the moment, bringing back all my memories of last night and the regret that comes with them. I blink and pull away, breaking the spell. Retreating is simply safer.

The bus trundles to a stop, and I follow Melanie off the bus. My car sickness was fake at first, but nausea is creeping into my throat as I stumble down the bus steps and onto the sandy path leading up to the temple. I take a huge swallow of air, which carries the light scent of salt water. We're high up on a cliff, where the temple stands at the top of a hill overlooking the ocean. The smell of the waves calms my churning insides.

Liam tucks his arm around my shoulders when he gets off the bus. "You okay?"

"Yeah," I say. I know he can see right through me, but I'm grateful when he doesn't push it.

Ms. Barlowe gathers us all by the ticket booth, and Ms. Galanis gives us some background on this land given to Poseidon long ago. The temple was built around 700 BCE, she tells us, and dedicated to the god of the sea. Amalia scribbles into her notebook, the cover pointedly angled so that no one can see what she's writing. As I watch her, I realize I'm not even sure what her project is about.

"So, let's go see it," Ms. Barlowe says, clapping her hands together. "This is one of the places I'm most excited about."

We follow her up the hill, dust kicking around my shoes with every step I take. I walk between Liam and Lucy, letting their conversation happen around me without my joining. Instead, I look up, pretending to be in awe of the sky.

I'm not pretending for long. We're climbing to the top of the promontory jutting out into the sea. The sky arcs above us before crashing into the ocean, surrounding us in a deep, all-encompassing blue. So many shades of the color collide together, creating a depth that fills me with the sudden yearning to throw myself into it.

Not in, like, a "jump off the cliff" kind of way. To be clear. I'm just suddenly struck by the desire to fold myself into the beauty of the world. To love the world and let myself be part of it.

And then we round the corner, and the temple comes into view.

The white marble columns stand on the rocky outpost, watching over the waves below. The sea extends everywhere beyond it. It's easy to see why anyone would choose this site to honor the god of the sea. This whole place would be a temple to Poseidon with or without the ruins standing watch over it. The columns reaching for the sky seem like a confirmation of something that was already true.

And I've spent my whole life, since I could read, learning as much as I could about the classics. But if I had to pick the moment I fell in love with them, truly all the way in love, I'd say right now. With the temple in front of me and the sea blazing with sunlight beyond it, I understand all the ancient stories for what they are—the living, kicking proof that people have been alive and loving the earth and trying to make sense of the world and their place in it as long as we have been here.

That's what these columns mean. I'm just joining my place in that ancient struggle.

"Holy shit," Liam says next to me.

All I can do is nod. Because yes. Absolutely. Holy shit, indeed.

Side by side, we make our way around the temple. Neither of us moves to take notes, so I know he's just as enraptured as I am. The meeting of these remnants of long-ago life and the natural beauty of this place are overwhelming in the best way.

"Can you believe these columns were put up literally more than two thousand years ago?" Liam asks as we pause to take them in.

I shake my head. "That's actually an absurd number. No way I can wrap my head around it."

People have been writhing over love and the agony of its loss for this long. The thought is the most comforting I've had in a while.

I just wish I could know what conclusions they drew.

For that, I suppose I can turn to the stories. I'm doing my project on Artemis, after all. *Her* conclusions on love are very clear: forsake it entirely and hunt in the woods with your friends by moonlight.

Sounds good to me.

We stay at the temple for a few hours. When we'd first seen it on the itinerary, that had felt like an oddly long time for one temple, but now that we're here, no one wants to leave. Liam settles himself on a huge rock to write presumably heartbreakingly good poetry in his journal, while Henry goes back to the bus to unload his painting supplies to capture the moment.

I still have no idea what I'm doing for this project, so I sit on a large rock next to Henry to watch him work. He told me once that he likes an audience. If I were as talented as him, I would too.

"I can't believe you're actually capturing how gorgeous this place is," I say, watching as his paint dots the canvas.

He grins. "I could never do that."

"I beg to differ." The colors he's flecking onto his painting perfectly mirror the way I feel about this place. "How's your trip going so far?"

I like Henry a lot. Both of us default to being the quiet ones in whole-cohort settings, but in the corners of time when it's just the two of us, it's easy to talk.

"Bro. So good." He gestures to the space in front of us, and I laugh.

"I *know*. It's unreal."

"But . . ." He trails off, his eyes tugged toward George, who's standing with his arms folded, deep in conversation with Bodhi.

"But?" I ask.

Henry sighs. "Sometimes I worry. I cannot deal with any more drama."

"Me neither," I say, exhaling with relief. At least I'm not the only one who's worrying about the group.

"This year has been pretty peaceful, so I thought we were okay," Henry says. "You missed the real headliners."

"I make my own drama well enough," I say, and he laughs.

"I just hope we're all still friends at the end of this."

"Me too," I murmur. This is why Lucy's focus on finding

everyone a romantic match is misguided, well-intentioned as she means to be. We should all focus on our friendships, on the bond we have as a group. Anything else is just a danger to that.

"Nothing's really happened so far, I guess," I say.

Henry nods slowly. "I just feel like we're putting weight on the cracks."

"That was the impression I got too, but Liam—"

"I love Liam, but he had rose-colored glasses on last time too." Henry sighs. "I mean, I love that about him. He sees the best in all of us. Anyway," he says, flicking his paintbrush and a spray of gold at me, "can you believe this place?"

"I actually cannot," I assure him.

It's true—sunset is blazing across the endless sky, gold and red lighting up the heavens. It's impossible to believe.

I let the view calm my racing brain, and for just a moment, the beauty of the world lulls it to quiet.

I will admit, I doubted Lucy's ability to sneak the entire co-hort out of our hotel for our last night in Athens. It seemed to me entirely implausible that she would manage to get us all out of there without Ms. Barlowe noticing.

But that's because I forgot the first cardinal rule of rule breaking: Always trust Lucy.

She faked an almost-midnight emergency so she'd have an excuse to roam the hallways, and she texted the group chat when she confirmed that the coast was clear. We left the hotel in pairs she pre-orchestrated so as not to alert the front desk that our entire school group had just left the premises, and we reconvened around the corner to make our way together to the nearest taverna.

The night air is still so warm, in a pleasant sort of way that feels absolutely antithetical to the New York City swamp summers I'm used to. The air is light and soft, a gentle heat that feels designed to be comfortable. We've all donned our finest summer wear for the occasion.

We make our way down our street, still lively this late into the night, until we reach a small taverna tucked into a corner. It's full of people, which seems promising, and a waitress is willing to find space for our huge group, which is ultimately all we need.

We gather around a few pushed-together tables, and Bodhi—who's been taking actual Greek lessons with a tutor while the rest of us lazily fumbled our way through Duolingo—orders for us. I catch only half of what he says, but it's enough to understand that he's gotten way too much food.

We swap our highlights of our time in Athens until our waitress returns, bearing so many plates of steaming meat, fish, and vegetables, it makes my stomach ache just to take in the sight.

"To our last night in Athens," Lucy says as we all take our first bites. "And to the rest of this trip. May it be fabulous. And bonding." She says this last part with a pointed look at Amalia, who tilts her eyes upward. "And very romantic, so we can all live our *Mamma Mia!* dreams."

For this last part, Lucy looks right at me. It's my turn to roll my eyes.

Instead of answering, I serve myself a heaping pile of horta, a dish of cooked leafy greens simmering in lemon juice. Like everything we've ordered, it's simple and straightforward, and I delight in the fresh crunch of the vegetables as I take my first bite.

"What if we all focused on our projects?" Henry mutters to me.

See? This is why I love him.

"Couldn't agree more," I say, nodding to Lucy.

She waves me off with her fork, bearing a juicy bite of bifteki. "You're being too secretive about your project for me to care about that."

"I'm not being secretive," I say. "I simply have no idea what I'm doing."

Lucy laughs at this. "Okay, fair enough. All the more reason to focus on romance."

"All the more reason to focus on my project, probably," I argue.

She shakes her head but digs into her food without arguing further.

"I have updates on the romance front," Amalia says with a grin.

George huffs disbelievingly. "Really?"

Lucy drums her fingertips against one another, looking at Amalia expectantly.

"Well, I met this adorable guy at the museum, because

I"—she pauses to give me a pointed look, and I narrow my eyes at her playfully—"know how to understand an assignment. And I had the most romantic date of my life last night."

Everyone at the table coos—except George, who rolls his eyes—as Amalia details her date. Her mystery man is a student at the University of Athens, and he showed her a rooftop terrace with a perfect view of the Acropolis at night.

At this, Liam shoots me a wide-eyed look. I can read right through the teasing grin plastered on his stupid face. *See? It's where locals take tourists on dates*, it whispers. I pretend I have no idea what he's trying to say, and I turn my attention instead to the horiatiki that's just made its way around the table to me. I've had Greek salad before, of course, but the freshness of these ingredients hits different here. I'm willing to pick my way around the feta if it means access to the juiciest tomato and crispest cucumber I've ever had in my life. And don't even get me started on the olives.

"That's cheating. Some of us are simply not suave enough to find dates at the museum," I point out.

"If only those people had romance options, like, right under their noses," Lucy says, and I aim a soft kick at her under the table.

"I think Bodhi and I should date," Liam says.

They tried this last year and, after three weeks of goofiness, decided they were made to be friends. Bodhi pretends to lean in for a kiss, and we all laugh.

"You wish," Bodhi says, tossing his long hair. "I'm taken and cannot participate in your summer games."

Lucy latches on to his arm and immediately begins pressing him for details, because the girl has no chill. I interest myself in finding the bottom of my plate of fried calamari. I was skeptical about the whole squid thing, but it took exactly one bite to convert me to the official biggest fan.

"So, what do we have to do to get you to date?" Lucy asks me when Bodhi finishes telling us about his new girlfriend, who he met touring a college campus in the spring. "I need to see it happen."

"I'll say," Liam mutters. I shoot him a murderous look.

"I'm not interested in dating," I say. This should be fair. This should be enough to shut down the conversation. Why do they keep pushing it?

"You're not interested in this summer being the best of your life? In finding your first love in the most romantic place on earth?"

And she's not *wrong*. But what business is it of hers?

"Okay," I say, fighting the smile tugging at the corners of my lips. "Fine. I'll find summer love."

Lucy cheers, punching two fists into the air.

"On three conditions."

Her fists plop back onto the table. "No fair."

"Yes fair," I say. "It's my romance. I should get to set the conditions, and you have to agree."

Lucy sighs. "Okay, okay. You're right. Tell us the three conditions."

"One," I say, holding up a finger, "she must make me feel at home while showing me new places."

This feels delightfully contradictory and wholly subjective. How can any of them prove that someone made me feel that way?

"Easy," Lucy says. "We're literally in a foreign country. Next."

I hold up a second finger. "She has to make me feel like myself while pushing me to grow."

It's impossible to feel this way, I imagine.

Amalia waves this off. "That's how any good love feels."

This throws me. It is?

I stare at her for a moment, trying to process her words. None of these conditions are filling them with the kind of hopelessness I was hoping to inspire. I need something so out of reach, they'll decide to give up right here and right now.

The idea comes to me in a flash, and I grin as I raise my third finger.

"She has to beat me in a footrace."

This is met with a chorus of booing, and I know I've won. Just like I won every track meet this year—and set a new school record for fastest time in the hundred-meter sprint.

There's no way they'll find someone who can do all three. And they know it.

Chapter Six

THE FERRY TO CRETE IS SO massive, I sort of wonder how it floats. I understand this is a stupid question, but the amount of metal involved feels implausible. The vessel is huge enough to fit a cavernous parking lot packed with cars and still have room for everyone to bunk for the night, dine at their choice of restaurant, and lounge on one of the decks.

Yet in spite of this wealth of solid ground to stand on, I still end up hanging over the side of the railing an hour into our trip, staring out at the horizon to ward off the seasickness building in my gut. I'm not sure if it's actually helping the roiling feeling in my stomach, but at least it's so breathtakingly beautiful that I can't focus on anything else. The Aegean glimmers too much beneath me, a kaleidoscope of all possible versions of blue colliding over and over in its depths.

The waters are clear and sun-warmed, an inviting mix that has me ready to dive off the boat. Not even as an escape from the seasickness, but just because its siren call is impossible to resist. Each new wave sends a spray of white froth forward that catches fire under the orange of the setting sun dipping toward the horizon.

Seasick or no, how could I take my eyes off it?

Liam, brave friend that he is, stands next to me, rubbing my back.

"You'd think a boat this big could handle a few little waves," I say, glancing down at the deep crystal water lapping at the edges of the boat.

"The boat can," Liam points out. "The boat is not the one having the issue."

I give him a withering look and go back to examining the horizon and inhaling deep lungfuls of salty air. The sound and smell of the sea are somehow comforting, even though the sea is also technically responsible for my current queasy predicament.

Well. No. The sea could never do such harm. I blame the boat.

"Can I ask you something?" Liam asks.

I glance at him. He's looking at me with his "worried big brother" look, the kind he puts on when he's concerned about a decision I've made and is choosing to lean unnecessarily deep into our ten-month age gap.

"Of course."

"What was up with last night?" he asks.

I sigh. "I just don't like it when people can't respect my privacy. If I say I don't want to date, that means I don't want to date. What business is it of anyone else's?"

Liam nods slowly. He wraps an arm around me, shifting so that his hands are resting on either side of me on the railing. I lean my head on his shoulder, and we stare out at the horizon together.

"That part is fair," he says. "Lucy can be . . . a little too willing to over-involve herself in other people's business."

"I'll say," I mutter.

"But she means well," he insists. "She cares about you, and we can both see that you're shutting yourself off from the world."

"I don't care that she means well," I say, ignoring the rest of his sentence. "It's still unnecessarily intrusive."

"I guess," Liam says.

I bristle at his skeptical tone. Liam is usually on my side with stuff like this. The petty cohort dramas are easy to get through when he, at least, always gets where I'm coming from. The idea that he might not approve of my choices is almost enough to make me rethink them.

Almost.

"Do you really think I should be forcing myself to date when I don't want to?" I ask him.

He shrugs, and I lift my head to take in his expression. His jaw twitches as he stares out at the sea.

"I just think you should ask yourself if it's what you really want," he says. "Not shut yourself down so much."

"I'm not shutting down," I argue. "I'm here. In Greece. With my friends."

"Yeah, and you've barely said a word the whole time we've been here," he points out.

I scoff. This is patently untrue.

Mostly.

"I've been talking just as much as I normally do," I argue.

"I'm just worried about you," Liam says softly.

I push off the railing, adding to the air between us. "No need to be. I'm fine."

Before he can say anything else, I spin away from him and storm around the ferry. The middle of the open outdoor deck is lined with plastic blue chairs, and there I find Melanie digging into a sandwich she got from the ferry's café.

"Hungry?" she asks when I reach her, holding out a bag of bagel chips.

I'm not, but a bagel chip sounds like it would taste better than the bitter tang of an argument with Liam, so I thank her and take one. She nods to the seat next to her, and I plop down into it.

"How's the seasickness?" she asks.

I'd entirely forgotten about the nausea that sent me to the railing in the first place. "Better than before. Thanks."

"I hate sleeping on ferries," she mutters. "I always get night seasick."

I grit my teeth. "I hadn't thought of that."

She pats my shoulder. "See you out here at midnight, I guess."

"Bagel chips and ginger ale?" I offer.

She laughs, and I ignore the yearning ache that the sound brings me. Just because I like to make her laugh doesn't mean that Liam and Lucy are right. They've inserted themselves so aggressively in the middle of my dating life, where they have no business being. I don't need to listen to a word they say.

Once we're armed with sandwiches and baked goods from the ferry café for dinner, Ms. Barlowe leads the entire cohort to an empty deck, where we take our seats and spread our food around us.

"Welcome to our first official decathlon event: the open mic night and talent show," Ms. Barlowe announces, standing in front of the rows of plastic seats we've taken. We cheer in response. "The event will be judged by Ms. Galanis and me and emceed by our very own Melanie."

She throws her hands out, gesturing for Melanie to join her on the makeshift stage. Melanie jogs up, leaving her half-eaten sandwich to cool on the blue plastic of her seat.

"Welcome, all, to my open mic night," she says, holding her phone to her lips as if it's a microphone. "I'm so excited to see what our gorgeous talent has planned for us this evening.

Can they do anything other than be nerdy about very old books? Only time will tell."

"I'll save you the time—they can't," Lucy calls from the back row, where she's set up camp with a spanakopita the size of her face. She's met with a round of playful booing from Henry and Bodhi in the front row, both of whom have planned comedy sketches they're highly invested in.

As Amalia kicks off the proceedings with a song from *Wicked*, I dig into my sandwich, filled to the brim with roasted vegetables between crisp slices of warm bread. The sandwich is comforting enough to take my mind off the fact that I'll soon be "performing" by running as fast as I can from one side of the boat to the other. I have interests outside of the classics, but there's only so far track-and-field will take me in the performance department.

A sudden gust of sea-cooled night air sends a shiver through me, and Liam wraps his arm around my shoulders. I lean into his warmth, taking another bite of sandwich. As I let my weight sink into him, I wonder why it feels so different with Melanie. Loving Liam is easy, even fresh off the heels of a disagreement. It never sets off any of my defenses—except the ones I have to give people when they assume we must be madly in love. I never find myself needing to prove that he's right for me. I just know that he is. At this point, he's proven that more times than I can count.

There's never been a hint of romance between us, so there's never been anything to fear.

That's the way it has to be with Melanie too, I decide as I watch her cheer for Amalia as the latter bows and heads back to her seat. It's the only way to make it through the summer with my heart intact.

I've seen the alternative. Giving in to romance has swallowed Lizzie whole, and all that's left of my sister is wedding linens, color schemes, and talking about how perfect her perfectly regular fiancé is. Andrea has spent half her college prep fretting about how she and her boyfriend will stay together with two hours of distance separating their college choices. Her entire first semester has been mapped out with road-trip days and nights away from campus before she's even had a chance to set foot on it.

That's not going to happen to me. Not if I have anything to say about it. I'm here to finish a solid project and embarrass myself in front of my cohort at this open mic night, not lose my entire personality to loving a girl because her smile makes me feel like a warm puddle of goo.

George is up after Amalia, and he delights us with a series of impressions of ancient Greek philosophers. Henry and Bodhi go next, and their sketch about Zeus having an affair with a Starbucks barista is worth all the hype they preceded the skit with.

Before I know it, it's my turn. I stride up to the stage, tossing my hair.

"That may have been funny," I tell Henry and Bodhi, "but beat this."

Melanie holds up her phone's stopwatch, and my heart

stutters at the sight. The brain gremlin piloting my neurons has the sudden urge to impress her. I shake off the thought as I make my way to one side of the deck. It's about ten yards across to the other side. As soon as Melanie shouts, "Go," I fly across, my sneakers hitting the wooden slats of the floor with a loud thud at every step. I collide with the white-painted railing on the other side just over a second later.

"I think we can all agree: very fast," Melanie says. Her proclamation is met with cheers from the cohort, and I grin as I make my way back to my seat. The easy camaraderie of the group makes even a night in this unfamiliar place feel comfortable, and I've almost forgotten that we're technically competing tonight. I just clap my way through Liam's karaoke performance and cheer alongside everyone else when Ms. Barlowe and Ms. Galanis declare Henry and Bodhi the undisputed winners of the night.

The rolling waves swoop deep in my stomach as I toss on the thin mattress. I'm on the top bunk of a tiny four-bed room, with Lucy asleep in the bed below me. Amalia's light snores fill the cabin from the bunk opposite.

I don't understand how either of them can sleep through this. The waves outside may be mild, but they're enough to pitch a tsunami in my gut. How am I supposed to go to sleep in these conditions?

Annoyed, I fling myself down the ladder and grab a sweatshirt from my suitcase, pulling it on as I slip out the door, careful not to wake any of my cabinmates. Maybe some salty nighttime air will fix me.

Remembering my conversation with Melanie, I make my way to the store. A crispy-bagel-chip situation would go a long way in settling my stomach. Melanie clearly had the same thought—when I get there, she's just ahead of me in line. She beams when she sees me and then blushes.

The pink creeping into her cheeks might be the cutest thing I've ever seen.

"I shouldn't be so happy that you're having a hard time sleeping," she says.

I grin. "Here to keep you company. Where would I be without our midnight treats?"

We buy our chips, and I follow her outside. It's cold out on the deck, the night air slapping the waves against the sides of the ferry, but Melanie had the foresight to bring the blanket from her bunk. She sits close to me, our thighs touching, so she can spread the blanket over both of us. I bravely ignore the heat of her body against mine. I'd sit like this with Liam or Lucy without giving it a second thought. It doesn't have to be any different with Melanie. This is my window to prove to myself that we can just be friends, that we can have a version of this summer where I'm close to her without having anything to fear.

Not even if it makes that now-familiar yearning ache explode in my chest.

She tears open the bag of bagel chips and props it between us. I snag a handful. She leans back, staring up at the night sky. We've settled close enough to the side of the boat that the lights from inside don't intrude much on our view of the stars. With the churning black sea meeting the inky sky, the darkness beyond the ship seems like it could swallow us whole. The constellations glint above it all, the glimmering pinpricks enough to light up the heavens. I let my head tip back to take the stars in. They're all-consuming, the sky seeming to envelop the entirety of the space around us. When I see them like this, away from the streetlights casting a heavy glow above New York, it's easy to understand why the ancients brought the sky to life with the stories they told about the shapes in the stars. For them, the sky was already alive.

"So, why are you along for the ride?" I ask. "Knowing how much of a nonclassics girl you are."

Melanie laughs. "I mean, I love art and all. Greece is my home, and I love its history. I'm just a science geek at heart."

The first word that springs into my mind in response is *hot*, which I stamp out as fast as I can.

"What kind of science?" I ask.

"Physics," she says. "I want to study astronomy, when it's finally my turn for college."

"Damn," I say, tilting my head up again to look at the stars. I went to a talk once about how the ancients viewed the sky, and the presenter showed a photo of what the sky used to look like from Earth—without all the lights that are now blocking our view. Even just the sight of it on a screen was sheerly awe-inspiring—an infinite number of stars, the Milky Way clearly banding its way through the sky. This night—under this sky—makes me feel like that kind of magic might be possible for me too.

I tell Melanie about the talk, and she grins.

"That's part of the obsession, to be honest," she says. "I love that humans have been staring at the stars since we've been here, trying to understand them."

"I get it," I say. "That's what I love about the classics too. All the ways humanity has been the same this whole time. And all the ways we've grown too. Nothing makes me more emotional than stuff like ancient art of people playing with cats."

Melanie laughs. "That's adorable."

And suddenly her hand is in mine again. Under the blanket, she quietly slips her fingers into mine. I freeze, my muscles tensing up for a moment. I have no idea what to do. The part of me that wants to run away screaming is losing in the face of her warmth, the light in her eyes.

I take a deep breath and relax into the moment. Nothing has to come of it. We're just two girls, holding hands under a blanket and a nightful of stars.

It's going to be fine.

"Being into science is cool," I tell her. "All my friends are art geeks of one kind or another."

"Science is just a different kind of geekdom," Melanie says. "Although we do have some pretty cool lab equipment."

"I don't know," I tease. "I've seen the goggles they make us wear in chemistry."

The image of Melanie wearing said goggles pops unbidden into my mind, and it occurs to me that they might actually be really cute.

"Hey, the goggles are adorable," Melanie says, and I laugh.

"I don't doubt it," I admit.

We fall into a companionable silence, staring out at the sea with our fingers intertwined. I meet her eye, and the contact sets off a flurry of sparks in my gut. Their crackling feels like a warning. An alert, screaming danger.

Her eyes flick down to my lips, and I fall into a panic zone.

Holding hands is one thing. It's plausibly platonic. But kissing?

This can't happen. Not here, not now—not *ever*. This isn't safe. I'm not safe here.

I have to go.

I fake a yawn, letting go of Melanie's hand to cover it. "It's getting late."

"Oh." She nods, blinking quickly to cover the surprised look in her eyes. "Yeah. We should get some sleep."

"Long day tomorrow," I say, folding the blanket off me and handing it back to her. "See you in the morning?"

"Yeah," she says. She's giving me a look like she's trying to read me but doesn't know how. I can't say I blame her. I'm not entirely sure how to read myself these days.

"Good night," I tell her. It's a quietly intimate phrase, and it feels nice saying it to her. Enough so that I find myself wishing I could let myself lean into the moment, lose myself in it with her.

But I know where that leads. So I give her a small smile and head back to bed, where I spend the rest of the night tossing, seasick, in my bunk.

CHAPTER SEVEN

LUCY IS UNFATHOMABLY BOUNCY THIS MORNING. I don't know how she managed to squeeze this much energy out of a night of sea-tossed sleep on the ferry, but she bounds off looking disturbingly bright-eyed. Liam and I linger at the back of the group. We're both sporting cute dark craters under our eyes, which I'm not above teasing him about.

"I'm just saying, you were very smug about not being seasick for someone who spent all night throwing up," I point out, and he groans.

The ferry docks in Heraklion, and we all file out onto the dock. From the ferry, we cram into a large van, shoving our suitcases under our feet, and shuttle off to the Palace of Minos at Knossos. I've been excited for this stop even though it's not strictly related to my project. It's a Minoan palace with its earliest parts built in 1900 BCE, which would be more than enough to wrap my head around, but it's also said to be the site of the Minotaur's labyrinth.

Henry is Icarus's hugest fan, so he tells the beginning of the story as the van trundles down the road toward Knossos.

"King Minos commanded Daedalus and his son Icarus to build an elaborate labyrinth under his palace to house the Minotaur," Henry says, putting his phone flashlight under his chin and waving his fingers spookily around his face. George giggles at his ridiculousness. "They obeyed and built a labyrinth so complex that Daedalus himself could barely find his way out when he had completed his task."

"*Metamorphoses*-coded," Liam says, nodding appreciatively as he cites the text from which Henry pulled that detail. "Nice."

"But King Minos feared that Daedalus would reveal the secrets of the labyrinth and thus prevent his yearly human sacrifices to the Minotaur. So he imprisoned them in a tower overlooking the sea."

I crane my head to peek out the window of the van at the sea. It's the same water that Daedalus and Icarus looked down on from their mythological prison, yearning for the freedom promised by the waves. The thought thickens in my throat.

"But they desired their freedom, because, obviously," Henry goes on. "Daedalus gathered feathers fallen onto their windowsill from birds' wings. He built wings fashioned from the feathers, the threads in their blankets, the straps in their sandals, and beeswax. Before they took off, Daedalus warned his son not to fly too close to the water, lest it soak the feathers and dissolve the wings, nor too close to the sun, as it would melt the wax, and the wings would fall apart around him."

Henry turns off his flashlight and tucks his phone back into his pocket, and a hush falls over the van. If there's anything guaranteed to make a group of classics students emotional, it's the fall of Icarus.

"But the joy of freedom and the delights of the world buoyed Icarus's spirits, and he could no longer bind himself to any cage. He soared as high as he could and did not realize the wax had melted until it ran hot down his arms, and the wings turned to feathers around him."

We all sit in heavy silence for a moment, and then Ms. Barlowe breaks us free by applauding. We join her, and Henry unwisely stands to take a bow as the van jerks to a stop. He flops onto his seat, and George thumps him on the back.

"The palace ruins also teach us a lot about the Minoan period," Ms. Galanis reminds us as we file out of the van. "It's remarkably well-preserved, and it has a lot to offer us. We'll spend the morning here and go to the Heraklion Archaeological Museum after lunch, where we'll see some of the artifacts that were uncovered from this site."

The air outside the van still carries the light smell of the sea, as well as the old smell of dirt and dust gathering from the palace ruins. It's quickly becoming my favorite combination.

I follow Liam and Lucy toward the entrance, half listening as Henry tells the story of Ariadne and the Minotaur. I'm a huge fan of Ariadne. She helped save Theseus from the Minotaur by teaching him how to fight it and how to escape the maze—and he thanked her by abandoning her on the island of Naxos a mere few days later.

She won, though, because the god Dionysus fell in love with her when he saw her asleep (likely thing for an ancient Greek god to do). Her crown became a constellation, so proof of her love glitters forever in the stars.

A tale of hope and inspiration for the romantically unfortunate everywhere.

I quicken my step to catch up with the rest of the group, but when I make my way into the site, everyone's already off in their own corners. Bodhi is scribbling in his notebook, earphones in to indicate that he wants to be alone. Liam is deep in his latest poem. Even Lucy, queen of wanting this to be a summer of togetherness, has disappeared into her books.

I pull out my own project materials, not wanting to be the only one looking like they're wandering aimlessly around these gorgeous ruins. Unfortunately, it only gives me the appearance of a purpose. Unlike my classmates, I still have only the loosest vision for my project. Something about Artemis, with a focus on her followers. Maybe sprinkle a few representations of the moon in there. Somehow.

It's nothing compared to the masterpieces everyone around me is putting together. Even Lucy's dissertation, which on the surface might not sound like it would give artistic genius, might end up in a peer-reviewed paper.

But I have to have *something* to show for my time here. Something more than just the sideways glances I keep stealing at Melanie, who looks as exhausted as I do from our shared sleepless, seasick night. Because there's not even anything to show for that. I keep making sure of it.

Even after we leave the palace to check into our hotel, everyone still seems completely immersed in their projects. We unload from the bus and into the hotel courtyard. It's a cozy, intimate space animated by the splash of a circular stone fountain set in the middle of the cobblestones. Little balconies equipped with breakfast tables line the building surrounding us, potted greenery exploding from their chipping white fences. The rich red-purples of a far-reaching bougainvillea plant frame the deep blue doorway as the plant climbs up the whitewashed walls of the building.

As Ms. Barlowe checks us in, I slide onto the bench set by the fountain and watch the water droplets spatter on the cobblestones at my feet.

Ms. Barlowe emerges from the front desk area holding room key cards. As she passes them out, she tells us that we're due back in the courtyard for our decathlon art show in half an hour. It's a reminder that makes me cringe. I have a series of printed photographs ready to go, but the results of this competition are preordained. None of us can top Henry's painting talent.

That doesn't stop everyone from bringing forth their best shots. We come back down to the courtyard to find it set up with easels along the sides. Ms. Barlowe directs us to our stations. I'm in a corner by the bougainvillea, which is exactly where I want to be. The flowers themselves don't have a particular scent, but the leaves smell fresh and clean, and the colors are so vibrant against the white walls that I hope some of their beauty rubs off on my photography.

On the other side of the fountain, Liam is setting up his poems, which he's copied onto posters he got from a local supply store and decorated with penciled doodles and colorful watercolor splotches along the margins. Bodhi has turned his poems into concrete poetry, the words linking to form images of the sites that inspired them. Lucy has, indeed, put the cast of *Mamma Mia!* on horseback as part of her contemporary frieze project. Even Amalia, whose work is always decidedly academic, has shown up with pages of her essay folded into origami animals reflecting the myths she's writing about.

Henry, of course, shows us all up with the two paintings he brings of Icarus and Daedalus in mid-flight. He's captured Icarus in the moments before his fall, when he's at his highest, soaring closer to the sun than ever. The joy on his face is darkened only by the foreboding shadows in the background, warning us of his height and the fall we know is to come.

"When you're set up, walk around the courtyard and take in everyone's art," Ms. Barlowe says. She and Ms. Galanis have already started their rounds, clipboards in hand.

I finish propping up my last photograph—a blowup of a shot I took of Hadrian's Library—and join Liam in the circle around the courtyard. A light evening breeze rustles my hair as we make our way by the fountain. The sky above us sinks into a deeper blue, fringed with the pink tint of the dying sunset.

"Everyone is so good," Liam whispers as we pass George's station, where he's set up fashion sketches of dress designs inspired by each of the twelve gods and goddesses and ancient Greek fashion.

Liam is the most anticompetitive person I know, but even so, his voice is tinged with intimidation. I can't say I blame him. As I look at the talent around me, the takeaway is nothing but amazement weighed down with the realization that truly, I don't belong here.

It doesn't help that Ms. Barlowe and Ms. Galanis are adding copious scribbles to their clipboard notes as they make their rounds. I flinch when they get to my easels, desperate to know what's coming out of their pens. Though everyone's trying to pretend that they're unbothered, I can see all the cohort's eyes flicking to our pair of teachers as they evaluate our work.

When Henry is declared the unsurprising winner, he's met with applause that feels polite compared to the cheers that echoed on our ferry open mic night. I'm sure I'm not the only one who's realized that he's now won two of our events. We all slump back to our stations to take down our art, no one making eye contact as we troupe inside with our pieces.

"Sure you don't want to come?" Liam asks me as he examines his hair in the mirror.

I nod. "I need to work on my project. I'm feeling so behind."

It's true that I'm behind, but not so true that I intend to

work on it tonight. I just don't have it in me to listen to any more prattle about how I should be *putting myself out there*. I like it in the hole of despair I've dug for myself. It's closed-in and safe, if a little dim.

Liam sees right through me, of course, but doesn't argue. I give him a grateful hug before he makes his way out the door.

The night hangs heavy and silent over the empty hotel room. I putter around it in silence, flipping aimlessly through my notebook and paging through one of books I brought with me until I crack and head down to the hotel lobby. At least there I can overhear snatches of conversations in Greek from my fellow hotel guests and watch the fountain in the courtyard splash onto the cobblestones around it.

I've just taken a seat in one of the big armchairs by the windows when I hear someone clear their throat behind me.

"My favorite fellow insomniac," Melanie says. "We meet again."

I grin at her. "Can't sleep?"

"Never," Melanie says with a groan. "You didn't want to go out with your group?"

"Needed a break," I admit. Self-consciously, I realize that she might've wanted to, though. "I'm sure you could've joined them if you wanted to. I can help find—"

"Lucy invited me," Melanie says, waving off my concern. "I felt a little too awkward to say yes. You're all so close, and I feel a bit like an intruder."

I wince sympathetically. "I'm sorry. We don't get out much outside of each other."

She laughs. "It's okay. My awkwardness in big groups is my burden to bear—not your fault. I was . . ." She trails off, staring into my eyes, and I try my best not to shrink under her gaze. It feels like she's trying to read me again. "I was thinking of sneaking off to this little beach nearby. It's unfathomably cute there. Do you . . . ?"

The end of her sentence falters, but I'm already nodding in spite of myself.

"Yes," I say. "Yeah, I'd love to. Sounds perfect."

"Okay," Melanie says, her shoulders relaxing. "Let's go."

Keeping Lucy's wisdom in mind, we slip out of a side entrance so that we don't invite the hotel staff to debate whether they should report our escape to our chaperones. Melanie promises that the beach is only a short walk away, and I follow her down the side of the dark road, flip-flops clapping with every step.

There's enough traffic that we can't walk side by side without risking our lives, so we stay single file as we make our way down. It gives me just enough time to wonder what I'm doing here. To mull over why I can't get myself together and pick a side. Do I want to run away from Melanie or toward her?

The two warring parts of my heart cannot agree about this girl with the dangerously deep eyes and the laugh that lights up her whole face.

Eventually, Melanie veers off the road and onto a narrow dirt path that cuts through a wild patch of tallgrass. We scramble down a steep ledge, large rocks offering themselves as footholds. I find myself on smooth sand stretching across a small crescent-shaped cove of a beach. Hidden from the road by the tallgrasses that line the upper ledge, we might as well be the only two people in the only place on earth.

Before us, the sea glitters as each wave catches the starlight. The rhythmic crash of water against land thrums with the peace of the world. The moon hangs above it all among more stars than I've ever seen in my life. The summer constellations wink down at us, the Milky Way a hazy band of light making its way across the sky. I exchange a wide-eyed look with Melanie.

"It's gorgeous here," I whisper, afraid that my voice will break the tranquil spell this place has cast on me.

"The best," Melanie agrees.

She makes her way to where the water meets the sand, and I join her. We let the waves rush over our feet. The water is clear and warm, and I wish I'd brought a bathing suit.

Melanie, I soon realize, has no such qualms. She peels off her shirt and shorts and slips right into the water. My embarrassingly frayed sports bra is a lot less put-together than the matching green situation she has going on, so I stay put.

Even in the crescent moon's light, I can see her eye roll.

"Just get in," she says, splashing water at me.

It's unbelievably warm, even at night, and the spray leaves me wanting more. Looking everywhere but Melanie, I slip out of my sundress and throw myself immediately into the next wave before she can take in any of what I—or my tattered bra—look like.

We swim out until our feet can't touch the sandy bottom

anymore, legs kicking to keep us afloat. The little waves lap at our shoulders.

"This might be the most beautiful place on earth," I tell her.

She smiles. "I knew you'd like it."

She looks unerringly beautiful, salt water dripping off her eyelashes and dark wet hair slicked against her shoulders. Her tan skin absorbs the moonlight, and her eyes reflect the skyful of stars.

I want to kiss her.

The thought comes unbidden and extremely unwelcome.

It's just the moment, I tell myself. The moonlight and the ocean and the two of us here, tiny dots in all this beauty. Kissing feels like it could belong in a moment like this. But *me* kissing *Melanie* belongs nowhere.

Or does it? a little part of me whispers. The war in my fast-beating heart rages on.

"I'm glad you're here." Melanie tips herself back so she can float on the water's surface.

"Thank you for bringing me," I tell her. "This really is the most beautiful . . ."

"I mean, here for the summer," Melanie says, staring up at the sky as she speaks.

"Me too," I say quietly.

I meet her eyes, as rich and dark as the night around us, and realize how much I mean it. Not just glad to be here, in Greece for the summer, but *here*, on this beach on this night, with her.

"I needed something good after this year," I mutter.

"What happened?" Melanie asks.

I kick the water around me to stay afloat, spreading my arms wide. They sway with the movement of the waves.

"My oldest sister got engaged in January, and my entire family lost the plot immediately," I tell her. "She used to be one of my favorite people. Now all she can talk about is wedding stuff."

This is factually true. It's not exactly what made this year so hard, though. That has more to do with my breakdown during midterms and my parents forcing me to start seeing Paige. The OCD label she slapped on me, which my parents clung to like a life raft keeping them afloat in the storm of my emotions, so tempestuous that not even they could handle it.

"Exhausting," Melanie says, shaking her head. "Wedding stuff is so hard to keep up with."

"It just completely swallowed her whole," I say.

"I get what that feels like," Melanie says softly. Her gaze shifts slightly so that it feels like she's looking past me at the rocky outpost toward the far end of the beach. "I had a breakup this year. I mean, it was because we both realized we were gay. So that really took the sting out of it."

I laugh. "That's sort of amazing, actually. Are you still friends?"

"The best."

"That's the most important thing," I say.

She surprises me by nodding. "Always."

No one ever agrees with my take on this. Everything about the way our society talks about romance says it should be the pinnacle of existence. Even the way Liam and I have to explain that we're not dating—"We're just friends!"—pisses me off. *Just* friends. As if friendship is automatically diminutive. As if our friendships are always supposed to play second fiddle.

"What's he like?" I ask her.

"Dimos?" She smiles. "He's impossibly kind. We've been friends for a few years, and dated for a few months. Mostly because it felt like everyone expected us to, you know?"

I nod, my chin dipping into the salt water. I'm no stranger to the constant lingering expectation that lifelong male and female friends are destined to date. It took Liam coming out for all our parents to finally let it go. (Even though I came out a full four months before him. Because men's desire is all that matters, right?)

"I know exactly," I assure her.

She nods. "You and Liam get the same thing?"

I roll my eyes, and she laughs.

"So fun to be a lesbian." I sigh.

She raises an eyebrow, a teasing grin playing at the corners of her mouth. "Isn't it?"

Her words cut through me, and my breath catches on my lips. With the moonlight in her dark hair, her eyes bright as they meet mine—yes, god. Yes, it's fun to be a lesbian.

"But before the breakup was hard," Melanie goes on. "Relationships are hard."

"Tell me about it," I say. Maybe she'd understand the goings-on inside my brain better than I've been giving her credit for.

"I just get so anxious, you know?"

I nod. I do know exactly what she means. How it feels to be consumed, constantly, by the anxiety that I'm with the wrong person, pursuing the wrong thing. How much easier it feels to just shut myself off from all of it.

"I'm a recovering people pleaser," Melanie confesses. "I always found myself worrying about what he thought of me when we were dating. If I was enough, if he was going to leave me. At the time, that felt like it'd be the worst thing in the world. I did so much to try to keep him close. It's honestly embarrassing to think about."

Ah. So anxiety can come in different flavors, after all. I can't imagine responding to my fears by clinging closer to someone. All they make me want to do is run far in the opposite direction, as fast as my track-trained legs can take me.

"That sounds tough," I murmur. "I know how all-consuming anxiety can be."

That much, at least, I can understand.

"It did help me realize that being a people pleaser isn't the selfless thing I thought it was," Melanie says with a shrug. "Like, the way everyone talks about it, I thought I was putting other people first and doing this good thing by thinking about their feelings. I knew it was hurting me, but it felt like at least I was helping others, you know? But when Dimos and I broke up, I realized that I hadn't been putting him first at all. I was just putting my need to be liked ahead of all my other needs, and all of his. It was self-serving, and it hurt him more than I realized at the time."

The water keeps lapping at my shoulders. Even with the dark of the night, the water is clear enough that I can see my feet kicking under me to keep me afloat. But still, the dark makes me feel hidden. It gives the night a safe quality that makes it possible for me to speak.

"I totally get what you mean," I tell her. "I'm never more self-centered than when I'm anxious about something."

It's a realization I came to when listening to Paige talk about relationships. Not that I'd ever admit this to her. But I realized how many times I didn't show up for Liam the way he needed me to, because I was too busy worrying that his sadness was actually about him being mad at me. I've made him reassure me that he's not mad so many times, it's practically a routine.

Paige said that's something we could work on together with her stupid exposure therapy idea. It always sounds great in the moment, but then the worry settles into my head, and nothing can bring me any relief until I pick at the scab of my own panic, check what's underneath, confirm no infection is rotting.

The waves have drifted us closer to the shore, and my toes brush against the sandy sea bottom. We inch forward until we can stand, the water lapping at our collarbones. I catch my breath, tilting my head back to stare up at the sky and the vastness of the stars until the water settles a cold under my skin.

It occurs to me that I'm swimming in brand-new waters, endlessly far away from my home. And yet I feel so comfortable here with Melanie beside me. The first of my conditions comes rushing back to me. *She must make me feel at home while showing me new places.*

I blink, shaking the water out of my eyes. It's not like these conditions were based on anything real. I just wanted my cohort off my back. So what if I feel so at home with Melanie? That doesn't mean we're soulmates. Besides, there were other conditions. I breathe a sigh of relief, satisfied with this logic.

Still, I'm ready to be out of this water. I nod toward the shore, and Melanie follows me back to dry land. The soft sand coats our wet feet as we put our clothes back on.

"Is there any worse sensation than wet denim?" Melanie asks, wrinkling her nose as she buttons her shorts.

I laugh. "None. You're unspeakably brave."

We walk back to the hotel, exchanging stories about what our schools are like. She goes to an American school in Athens, and our experiences of high school aren't as different as I might have expected.

"Well," she says when we reach the side entrance of the hotel, pausing to meet my eyes.

I smile. "Thank you for this."

She nods. "Thank you for joining."

"Good night," I say quietly, and we part ways when we reach the hallway.

I make my way quickly back to my room, my hair dripping salt water down the back of my dress. When I swing the door open, I'm met by Liam, who looks up at me in confusion.

"I thought you said you weren't going out tonight?" he says, taking in my wet hair and sandy feet.

I shift my weight, looking down at my toes. "I . . . ran into Melanie, and she pitched . . . going out."

I'm not sure why I feel the rush of guilt that courses through me. I didn't intentionally hide our plans from him. They didn't exist until after he'd already gone out with the rest of the cohort.

Maybe it's just that I was hoping to keep my night out with Melanie to myself. Not a secret. Just . . . private. Something for me to hold on to, that I don't need to share with anyone else.

Too late for that now.

"Nice," Liam says, a note of confusion in his voice. "Did you go . . . swimming?"

"We went to the beach," I say, reaching for a towel hanging on the half-open bathroom door to wrap my salty hair. "Went for a quick swim."

Liam moves to his twin bed, flopping back onto it. "You and Melanie?"

This he says with a lighter, teasing tone that makes me want to shrink away.

"Yes," I say curtly. "Me and Melanie."

He lifts his head to meet my eye. "You okay?"

I nod. He means well. We can usually tell each other anything, and he's always been able to ask me things I wouldn't ever want to admit to anyone else. But today I want to hold this moment close to my heart, where I can figure out what it means for myself before I share it with anyone else.

"You?" I ask. I can't shake the feeling that he's mad at me

for ditching plans with him only to hang out with Melanie instead.

"Of course," he says. "We found the cutest patio and people-watched. And cat-watched. There are *so* many cats here."

He pulls out his phone to show me the series of strays that walked by, hoping for a bit of the fish he'd ordered. I lean over to look, swallowing the fear bubbling up in my throat.

He tilts the phone slightly away from me, and my heart rate picks up. I scan him from out of the corner of my eye, looking for other signs that he might be pissed. His eyes stay fixed on his phone, as if he can't bear to look at me. Is he angry with me? I close my eyes, trying to take a deep breath, and the end of our friendship flashes under my eyelids. Is he? My thoughts tighten their circle, spinning faster and faster, the urge to ask him building ceaselessly in my throat.

Don't ask don't ask don't ask don't—

"Are you mad at me?" I blurt out. The moment the words fall from my lips, the moment I move to check, my whole body calms.

He shakes his head, glancing at me. "Of course not. Why would I be?"

I reach for my pajamas and duck into the bathroom to get out of my wet things and into an oversized T-shirt stolen from Lizzie. A leftover from her era of being cool.

I brush out my hair, meeting my eyes in the mirror. Barely any time has passed since I asked, but the worry about Liam bubbles in my throat again. I swallow it down and force myself to brush my teeth. There's enough to worry about as it is.

It's still dark out when the hotel phone rings. Liam groans, his hand fumbling across the nightstand as he refuses to open his eyes.

I echo his whine. "It's way too early for the wake-up call."

"Mistake," Liam howls as he picks up the phone, but he falls silent as he listens to the other end.

"Tell them we're going back to bed," I mumble, rolling back over.

Instead, he says, "See you soon."

He hangs up, and I turn to glare at him blearily, my eyelids drifting shut in spite of my fury. "Bro. What part of need more sleep is not—"

"It was Melanie," he says.

My eyes snap open. "What did she want?"

He wiggles his eyebrows as he switches the lamp on, and I roll my eyes.

"What?"

"She wants to take all of us on a sunrise hike," he says, throwing the blankets off him and bouncing out of bed. His ability to go from asleep to awake in less than ten seconds is seriously disturbing.

"All of us?" I croak out, my voice heavy with my exhaustion. I wonder if Melanie would've preferred if our beach trip last night had been a group outing. The thought makes me want to go back to sleep and stay asleep for the rest of the trip.

"All of us," Liam confirms. He's somehow already dressed and is running his fingers through his hair. "You ready?"

I stare at him, my hair clouding in front of my eyes. "I am still in bed."

"A state you should change. Quickly," he says, nodding to the door. "She's leaving in ten minutes."

I hoist myself out of bed and into a pair of leggings. It's too late to do anything about my hair except to force it into a ponytail that immediately gets messed up by the sweatshirt I add as we head out the door.

We meet Melanie in the hallway by the side entrance. She somehow looks amazing. Her skin is glowing as if she's gotten a full night of sleep, and her eyes brighten when they see me.

Does that mean she was glad it was just the two of us last night, after all?

Or is she just being polite?

And why do I even care?

It's a lot to process at five in the morning. I take a bite of the crumbly granola bar I found in my airport backpack, hoping it has enough calories to fix me. At least for the morning, if not forever.

"Y'all ready?" Melanie asks.

The whole cohort is assembled in various states of readiness. Bodhi is the only one who looks like he's actually prepared for a hike. Lucy and I are at the other end of the spectrum as the groggiest people alive.

Melanie opens the door, and a burst of cool early-morning air greets us. I take a deep breath as soon as we step outside. The sea flavors the air even this far out. I exchange glances with Melanie, and she smiles at me. I wonder if she's also thinking about the cool water last night, the way we looked at each other under the crescent moon.

"So ready," Amalia says. She's even brought her notebook.

We follow Melanie to the trailhead, which is tucked away behind an overgrown hedge on the side of the road near our hotel. It's still dark, though the sky is starting to lighten, tinges of yellow announcing the coming sun.

As I try to keep up with the group, all my anxieties from last night come rushing back to me. Plus a few extra. I don't know if I should walk by Liam to make up for how I ditched him last night, or if Melanie was hoping I would hike with her. Or if I should be staying far, far away from both of them, due to how furious I'm sure Liam is with me and how painfully awkward Melanie probably thinks I am.

Never mind how confusing it is to figure out how *I* feel in all this.

It's all enough to make me out of breath. Throw in the gradual uphill slope of the hike, and I'm panting as I struggle to keep up with the group, anyway. No need to overthink after all.

The hike reminds me of our scramble down the small ledge last night. We're walking up a dirt path, rocks heaped in our way. Tallgrasses line the path on either side, filling the air with the scent of dry greenery. I gasp in lungfuls of it, trying to hide how out of breath I am from the rest of the group.

Mercifully, Melanie has pulled us for a short hike. It's barely been half an hour by the time we reach the top of the hill. It opens onto a grassy clearing that overlooks the sea, a few large rocks resting in the warm dirt of the earth. I clamber up one and sit cross-legged on top of it, watching the sea. The first rays of sun are already transforming the sky, flaming red streaks dancing at the edges of the horizon. We're all quiet as we watch the sun blaze into the morning, the sea reflecting the golden start of the day.

"Damn," Lucy says when the brilliant oranges have tamed into early-morning yellows. "That was incredible."

"Thanks, Melanie," Liam says, nodding.

She grins. "Thought it'd be worth it."

"Definitely," Bodhi agrees.

"Sadly, I have to pack," Liam says, getting up from the rock he'd perched himself on. "My suitcase exploded overnight somehow."

"A mystery," George quips.

"You coming?" Liam asks me, pausing in front of my rock.

I glance at Melanie, who's still staring out at the horizon. "I might stay a little longer. Catch my breath."

Liam shrugs and nods, and if he sees through me, he doesn't say anything. Everyone slowly filters out of the clearing and back down the hill to the hotel, until it's just Melanie and me, sitting in the stillness of the morning, watching the dawn.

MOM: I called Paige this morning, and she says she hasn't heard from you all summer. Is everything okay?

NATALIE: Yes

NATALIE: Hence why I have not needed to talk to Paige

MOM: Maybe try to make time for a check-in. It can't hurt! xoxo

Chapter Eight

ANOTHER DAY, ANOTHER FERRY. THIS ONE shepherds us from Crete to Paros after a few days on the big island, and we spend the ferry trip performing our speeches as our next decathlon competition. If I thought the vibes were tense at the art show, they're nothing compared to the applause we're giving one another now. Everyone's written a two-minute speech about their research. I fumble through mine, so the smattering of tepid applause isn't a surprise, but everyone's turn is met with similar lukewarmness.

When Liam is declared the winner, I hear George and Bodhi grumbling to themselves. We spend the rest of the ferry ride buried in our books. Getting off the ferry and onto sweet, steady land is a relief.

We're stopping by the Archaeological Museum of Paros,

as well as a historic church, but Ms. Barlowe has promised that the next few days are our designated beach-and-chill time.

"We're going to give you some independent work and explore time" is how she actually phrased it. But we're all well-trained in the fine art of translation.

So as soon as we check into the hotel, we dump our stuff and head straight for the beach. Lucy and I spend the day side by side, asleep on beach towels, and I'm rewarded with a smarting sunburn across the backs of my shoulders by the end of the day.

Worth it. Best sleep of my life.

I'm rooming with Amalia in this hotel. Ms. Barlowe thrives on keeping us on our toes by reconfiguring the rooming arrangements now and then. Amalia, who actually spent the day working on her project, conks out moments after dinner. I'm restless from my blissful day of napping, though, and before long I find myself wandering the hotel lobby. Totally aimlessly.

The fact that I'm wearing my favorite sundress and glancing up hopefully every time I hear footsteps coming down the hall is a total coincidence.

Eventually, she shows up. I can feel my face brighten when I see her, and the realization makes me blush. She smiles when she sees me, and I will the red blotches to drain from my cheeks.

"Couldn't sleep?" I ask, a rush of nerves fluttering through me as she takes a seat next to me.

She shakes her head. "Hoping for a more fun evening than that."

I bite my lip, dropping my gaze to hide it from her eyeline. The idea that an evening with me sounds like fun to her makes my head spin.

Not that she necessarily came here in search of me. Not everyone is as embarrassing as I am. But at the very least, she doesn't seem to mind folding me into her plans.

"Anything particular in mind?" I ask.

"I have a friend who lives on the island. His dad is a fisherman. Which means . . ." She trails off, giving me a secret smile.

"He has a boat," I realize aloud.

She nods. "He has a boat."

The boat is tiny and smells of fish. The blue-and-white paint cracks along the side, and the wood along the railing threatens splinters at every turn.

I immediately fall in love with it.

"He said we could use this one," Melanie says as she hops aboard. She gives me a nervous glance. "I'm sure you can see why he's willing to risk it."

"It's perfect," I assure her, meaning it. Floating with her in the Mediterranean aboard this rickety boat full of old charm is peak romance.

Platonic romance, I mean. To be clear.

I think.

The thoughts swirl so much, they threaten to rock the

boat. They don't even feel like they belong to me or that they come from me. They come to me from somewhere else, like a swarm of bats descending on my brain and obscuring the parts of me that know how to think, how to interpret my own feelings. All I can do is let the questions chase themselves into exhaustion.

Do I like her? Is it pointless to fight it? Will it ruin everything if I don't? What am I supposed to do? How do I know what's right?

All this courses through me relentlessly, but I'm just sitting quietly on the wood bench carved into the wall.

I force myself to smile at Melanie as she starts the motor.

"When did you learn to drive a boat?" I ask, not even trying to hide how impressed I am.

"Spending summers here with Nick," she says. "Our dads were childhood friends, and they basically forced us to be childhood friends too. Not that it took much forcing," she adds with a grin. "He's really cool."

We drift away from the dock, the water rippling in our wake.

"So, you spent your summers here growing up?" I ask. I'm curious about her life, how mini-Melanie spent her days. All the things she experienced that led her here. I realize I want to know them. I want to know *her*, all the way.

"Not all summer every summer," she says, "but we usually made the trip for at least a couple of weeks. It was always a highlight of the summer, though. I'd help on the boats. Well"—she laughs—"probably I got in the way. And we'd eat our weight in loukoumades every night."

"Loukoumades?" I ask.

"Oh my god, we have to get some while you're here," she says as she steers the boat out of the little harbor. We're still staying close to the island, navigating around the lit-up port. The small town twinkles in the night. "They're sort of like honey doughnut holes, and they're magical."

"That sounds magical." I sigh. "The food here is really living up to Ms. Barlowe's extensive hype."

She grins. "Tell that to my mom. She grew up in New York, and sometimes I think she'd kill for access to Chinese food."

"How did I not know she grew up in New York?" I ask. She's Zoomed with us weekly all year, and it's never come up that she was a fellow New Yorker.

Melanie laughs. "I think she wants to preserve an aura of authenticity for your class. Imposter syndrome runs in the family."

"What's your strand of it?" I ask.

The dull sound of the motor rousing the water fills the space between us. Melanie shifts her weight in the driver's seat so she can cross her legs beneath her.

"I guess, since I have so many older friends, it's easy to feel like I'm falling behind, in addition to being left behind." She glances at me. "You said . . . I don't know. Does it ever feel that way to you?"

I've always felt awkward describing my feelings of inadequacy as imposter syndrome. Because that's for people who *are* good and just don't know it. I'm actually worse at this than all my classmates. There's no syndrome; I'm just an imposter.

"It's definitely been weird being the only freshman this year," I admit. "And I don't think there are any incoming freshmen joining the program next year, so I'll still be the baby. As per usual."

"How's your sister's wedding planning going?" Melanie asks with a coy smile.

I roll my eyes. "It's managing to haunt me even all the way over here. I'm going to be wearing blue."

"You'll look amazing," Melanie says, her voice low. I meet her eye and immediately find myself pulled into the intensity of her gaze. I want so badly to let myself be drawn into her, to follow this moment wherever it could lead.

But this time she's the one who pulls away from it first. She blinks, and her eyes land back on the steering wheel.

"We should head back," she says quietly, almost to herself.

I glance at the town as she brings the boat around. This shift in Melanie's demeanor brings a whole new set of fears crashing through me. Have I waited too long to decide, and now the option is off the table? Does she feel like I led her on, and now she doesn't want to even be my friend?

Plus, Liam is still mad I ditched him for her, probably, so it's suddenly feeling like there's a good chance I'm going home with no friends at all.

It doesn't help when I realize, with a sinking feeling in my gut that has nothing to do with the lurching of the boat, that stealing a boat ride was on his bucket list. Something we were supposed to do together. If there's a decathlon event for worst friend of the summer, I'm winning for sure.

The motor keeps sputtering as Melanie turns the boat, spinning a wide arc back toward the harbor. I bring my knees to my chest and wrap my arms around my lower legs, trying to keep myself together somehow. My thoughts spin and spin and have lost their spot, rendering me a dizzy mess. I know I have to get it together, but I have no idea *how*. Paige loves to make all these suggestions, but they always make me feel like she has no idea what she's talking about. How is telling myself that *maybe* I'll have no friends when I go home supposed to help me right now?

"You okay?" Melanie asks.

I jump, startled by the reminder that there's someone else here. That I'm still on the boat, the cool night air rushing past my cheeks and the water propelling us forward under a blanket of stars, that I'm not in a dark vortex of panicked incoherency.

"Yes," I manage to get out. "I'm fine."

Melanie nods, but I can feel her eyes on me as we reach the harbor and I help her retie the boat to the dock. Once she's satisfied that the boat is secure, we make our way to the hotel. I'm itching to get back to the way things felt on the boat, when it seemed like anything could happen. Like it was just the two of us, held close by the warm darkness of the night. But I'm afraid of how quickly she shifted. I'm not sure how to read it except to think that all my worrying has made itself a moot point because any potential for romance has been taken off the table.

The hotel comes into view before I've figured out how to

put my scrambled brain waves into coherent thoughts, let alone words. When we reach the lobby, she surprises me by pulling me into a hug. For one brief moment, I am engulfed by her. She smells like cinnamon conditioner and salt water, and her warm exhale fans across my shoulder. It's enough that, for the time I'm in her arms, my brain turns off, and I can just let myself be.

But then she pulls away, and the noise of the day comes rushing back into focus.

"Good night," she says with a sleepy smile. "Thanks for coming out with me."

"Are you kidding?" I ask. "Thank *you*. That was incredible." My eyes linger on hers, wanting to let myself melt into them but struggling to read her expression. What is she thinking? It's impossible to make out any kind of explanation in the depths of her irises. I swallow and take a step back toward my room. "Good night."

When I get back to my room, I realize I missed a text from Liam—first to me and then in the group chat.

> LIAM: wanna hang tn?

No-Murder Secret History

> LIAM: Anyone up for a night out?

> LUCY: always

I'm relieved he was able to hang with Lucy, but I can't evade the pinpricks of guilt that crawl spidery in my gut. It only doubles when I remember that riding a boat was on his— *our*—bucket list. I've ditched him twice in just one night.

And he's already angry with me.

Our friendship feels like it's clinging to the edge of a cliff, its fingers slipping off the rocky rim. I text him back, leaving out where I actually spent the evening. It's not technically a lie, but it only makes me feel worse.

> NATALIE: So sorry, just saw this!! I'm the worst. Hope you had fun with Lucy!

> LIAM: I did! But I miss you!

> NATALIE: Miss you too

> NATALIE: Let's hang tomorrow?

> LIAM: Yes please!

The guilt prickles at the corners of my eyes. I swipe at them as I change into my pajamas and tuck myself into bed. Amalia's light snores fill the darkness of the room, but even with the reminder of her company, I've never felt more alone.

CHAPTER NINE

MY MOM ALWAYS LOVES TO SAY that things will look better in the morning. I spent my childhood trying to argue with her about that. I was prone to nightmares as a kid, and no assurances that morning would eventually come could ease the frantic distress that came with bedtime.

I'm reminded of her words now, watching the early-morning sunrays ease through the translucent white curtains framing the windows.

The situation does seem easier now that daylight is shining on it. I'm going to make things right with Liam today, make it all up to him. As for Melanie—her new hesitancy is for the best. My focus is supposed to be on Liam, on the competition. How many times do I have to tell myself that romance will just suck all the life out of everything?

I throw the light comforter off me and toss myself out of

bed, flinching as the soles of my feet meet the cold floor. I hop my way to the bathroom on the balls of my feet and change into my beach outfit. Today's the day to break out my favorite blue bathing suit, which I cover with a gauzy green wrap my mom splurged on when she found out I was going to get to spend the summer in Greece.

Having the wrap fall on my shoulders now makes me feel closer to her, and a sudden wave of homesickness washes over me. For the first time since I got off the plane, I feel the distance between home and where I am now, like there's a rope keeping me linked to my house and a heavy weight has just been set on the rope, straining me downward.

I check the family group chat, which I muted a couple of days ago to escape yet another spiraling argument fueled by Lizzie's anxiety. There are hundreds of messages to catch up on, most of them related to the aforementioned argument. Andrea pops in every once in a while to ask questions like *Where's my blue blazer?*, which seem to invite follow-up questions along the lines of *Why wouldn't you walk out of your room to ask Mom out loud?*

There is a conspicuous lack of anything like *How's Natalie doing so far from home?* The only time I come up directly is when someone is wondering about Paige.

Have they even noticed I'm gone? Or have I fallen so far behind the rest of them that it's easy to leave me behind?

I think about sending a few photos from the trip, but the possibility of them being drowned out by Lizzie's latest wedding stress stops me. I toss my phone into my beach bag with perhaps more force than is necessary. Slinging the tote over my shoulder, I leave the bathroom and slip into my flip-flops before heading to the breakfast room.

Even amid all the problems I've created for myself in my own head, I have to pause to admit that this beach has to be the most beautiful place on earth. It's larger than the one Melanie took me to in Crete. The clean, soft sand stretches lazily until it reaches a rocky ledge, huge seaweed-slicked black rocks rising out of the sand and crashing into the sea. Each wave douses them with a spray of white froth. Where we are, the water is clear, a shimmering turquoise at the edge of the sand that transforms into a magnetically deep blue as my eyes drift outward to the horizon. There the clear sky dips into the sea, holding us close in this wide, peaceful space.

This whole trip has us gorging ourselves on the beauty of the world—natural and human-built. I sit up on my towel, my fingertips drumming against the sun-warmed sand, and drink it all in. The little waves lap at the soft sand, each one much the same as the one before it, but I could never get tired of watching them.

Liam is laid out on a towel next to mine. My immediate sunburn is a cautionary tale he's heeded—we've only been here for an hour, and he's already reapplied sunscreen along his shoulders twice.

"Want to go in?" he asks, opening one eye to meet mine.

I look down at him, shading my eyes with my hand. "Eventually."

Though the warm clarity of the water is tempting, the heat of the sun on my skin is too nice to change for now. I let its rays wash over me, not even minding where they smart at the fading lines of my sunburn.

The rest of the cohort is spread out around us. Even Melanie joined today, though she's spent most of it in the water. But even though the group is technically here together, we don't feel like the cozy unit we usually are. There's no overlapping chatter, no one yelling over one another or carrying on three different conversations at once. Half of us are buried in books, even at the beach. The other half are sitting in mostly silence, a stack of closed books quietly nagging at us from the corners of our towels.

I'm in the latter group. My research materials—including several paperback editions of Anne Carson's poetry that probably count more as pleasure reading, as they are not, strictly speaking, related to Artemis at all—collect sand in their pages from their places weighing down the sides of my towel. Still, I don't move to pick any of them up. Instead, I watch Henry paint the waves. Seeing them through his eyes, his deft fingers capturing the way each wave glimmers in the sun, only makes them more beautiful.

"Should we play a game?" I ask when the awkwardness of the silence becomes too heavy to stand. "I have some rackets."

Turns out, the only thing more awkward than the silence that came before my question is the one that comes after it.

"Maybe later," Bodhi says after a beat. He's in the middle of writing a poem, so fair enough.

But then Lucy, who's not doing anything, just shrugs a shoulder. "I should really focus on my work."

Amalia only lifts her notebook in response, without pausing her scribbling for even a moment.

"Bad luck," Liam whispers to me. I sigh at him.

"What's gotten into everyone?" I hiss back. "Are we not here to have the best trip of our lives? *Together?*"

He gives me a look, one I can only interpret as "You have hardly been Ms. Team Bonding yourself lately," and I duck my eyes.

"It's the decathlon," Liam says, dropping his head back onto his towel. His curls fan out around him. "No one knows how to chill when there's a competition afoot."

"Afoot?" I tease, and he flicks my shoulder.

"Afoot," he confirms.

"Well," I say, nodding to the waves, "wanna come in with me?"

He bounces to his feet faster than I can process his reaction.

"I thought you'd never ask," he says. "Let's get in there."

He offers me his hand, and I let him help me up. The sand is hot underfoot, and we rush to the waves. Liam is a run-right-in kind of person, and he disappears under the water as if someone is in hot pursuit.

I prefer to let the waves lap at my ankles for a while, appreciating the warm gentleness of the water. That is, until Liam sends a splash my way.

"Get in," he whines playfully.

I groan at him but dunk myself into the water. The rush of water momentarily drowns out my thoughts, and I linger under the surface until the salt stings my squeezed-shut eyes. I break back onto the surface, inhaling deeply.

"Best ever, right?" Liam asks, floating next to me.

I nod. "Could've done without the splashing, though."

He splashes me again, and I dunk him under the water. He sputters as he emerges.

"No fair," he says.

I scoff at him. "Objectively, so fair."

"Yeah, you're right," he says, rearranging himself so that he's floating on his back. I join him in the same position, and we float side by side, staring at the sky.

"So," he says, and I can hear him wiggling his eyebrows in the corniness of his tone, "were you with Melanie last night?"

I lift my head so he can see me roll my eyes.

"That's such a reasonable question," Liam protests.

"It's the tone I object to," I tell him, "not the question."

"The tone is excessively reasonable," Liam argues. "You've been spending so much time together."

"You and I spend so much time together," I say. I regret it immediately. I've handed him the perfect opening to point out that we haven't been spending much time together at all now that I'm ditching him for Melanie right and left. I scan his face for signs of upset but find none. Perhaps he's becoming a very good actor. "That doesn't mean we're in love."

"There are some key differences," Liam points out.

"Oh, what, so we've established that a man and a woman can be friends, but two lesbians can't?" I reply hotly.

Liam stands in the waves, water dripping from his shoulders.

"Of course two lesbians can be friends," he says. "Just maybe not two lesbians who look at each other like *that*."

"Like what?" I ask, barely squeaking out the question. Is it that obvious?

"Like you're madly in love with each other."

"I barely know her," I scoff. He opens his mouth to argue, so I duck under the water again. It's salty and I can't breathe, but I'd take that over this conversation any day. Besides, there's peace to be found here. The water dulls my senses, cocooning me in a warm stillness that quiets my brain for a moment. I linger as long as I can.

Eventually, though, my lungs protest, and I'm forced back to the surface.

"Very mature," Liam says as I gasp for air.

"Anything to escape these accusations," I tell him.

He laughs. "I'm not accusing you of anything. I'm trying to help you see what you refuse to see on your own."

"What difference does it make how I feel?" I ask. "I know how I want to act. That matters more than anything, surely."

"But," Liam says, eyeing me, "do you?"

He has me there. Every time I'm around Melanie, everything I think I've decided turns sideways. It's no wonder she shied away from me last night. I've been taking steps forward and backward, as if I'm dancing my own private waltz on the head of a pin. Who could follow it when even I'm not sure I know the steps?

"Exactly," Liam says, correctly interpreting my silence. "You're a fresh disaster these days, Nat."

"Well, the scrutiny isn't helping," I snap. I take a breath, immediately regretting my tone. "Sorry. It's just . . . been hard."

"Sorry," Liam says, wincing. "That came out harsher than I meant it to. I just want you to be happy. And to be fair to yourself."

I stare out at the horizon. The water stretches on seemingly forever. The thought of floating here, in something so vast, is oddly comforting. It hits the same spot of my heart that loves thinking about how far back humanity—with all our quirks—stretches into history. I'm a little part of that like I'm a little part of floating in this endless water. Struggling with romance, making sense of love—I know from the stories I've studied that I'm hardly the first to deal with this.

It doesn't make it easier. But it does help a little. If even the gods messed it up, how can I expect my fifteen-year-old self to get it right at every turn?

"I want the same thing for you," I say, eyeing Liam. "So, where are your romantic prospects?"

Liam snorts. "I have none."

"So . . ."

"Not having any is different from running away from real

feelings you actually have because you're projecting your made-up fears onto real situations."

Ouch.

"That actually sounds super similar," I tease, and he splashes me again.

We're interrupted by Melanie herself, who floats over to us with eager eyes.

"Natalie," she says, and my name sounds thrilling on her lips, "I just had the greatest idea. Aren't you doing your project on Artemis?"

"Yeah," I say, though *doing* is perhaps an exaggeration.

"Delos isn't far from here," she says. After a beat, she bobs her head. "Well. It's sort of far, but we could totally do a day trip there. I'd be so down to come with you, and I'm sure Ms. Barlowe would say yes to an excursion if I was acting as a guide."

Delos is the mythic birthplace of Artemis and her twin brother, Apollo. Going there might be just the thing to jump-start my project. It needs the help—badly.

Of course, it's yet another thing that Liam and I said we would do together. But when I glance at him, he's nodding.

"That's such a good idea. Nat, you should go ask Ms. Barlowe right now."

I grit my teeth. He just wants me to go with Melanie because he's hoping I'll succumb to my feelings. No such luck for him. I'm going for my project and my project only.

Still, I agree. Because, like, I do need to go.

"Okay, I'll pitch it to her," I agree. "Thanks, Melanie."

She smiles. "I'm just here to make the most out of this trip, to be honest. I'll take a free trip to Delos any day."

We wade out of the water and back onto the sand, finding that Ms. Barlowe and Ms. Galanis have just returned from their morning of touring the island to let us have our beachy freedom. The itinerary for tomorrow is much the same, so a day trip away will have to be okay on those grounds.

But before I can pitch it to her, Ms. Barlowe calls us all to her. She's met with a few half-hearted groans as everyone shifts off their sun-soaked blankets to stand in a circle around her. I join the cohort, wrapping my towel tight around me. My hair drips salt onto my shoulders, and sand clings to my wet legs.

"We're going to have what I think is my favorite of the decathlon events," Ms. Barlowe says. "The beach games! We'll need you in two teams that Ms. Galanis and I have formed."

I end up on a team with Liam, George, and Lucy. Bodhi, Amalia, and Henry face off opposite us, with Melanie joining their team to round out the numbers.

"How will this work for the points system?" Amalia asks.

"Everyone on the winning team will get five points," Ms. Barlowe tells her. "But try to just have fun with it."

If the goal was fun, they shouldn't have put Amalia and George on opposing teams. Our first game of cornhole is quickly declared a wash after the beanbags get thrown too aggressively by both sides, resulting in a 100-percent miss rate and sand sprayed on everyone's shins.

We move on to potato-sack relay-racing along the waterline. I'm facing off against Melanie, and the two of us share wry grins as Ms. Galanis counts down the start of the race.

"May the best potato win," Melanie says, then takes off when Ms. Galanis shouts "Go."

I hop after Melanie, my legs hampered by the rough material of the sack. Losing a race is not something I do often, and the finish line feels far away, firing up my competitive instincts. Thighs burning from the effort, I heave my body forward with each leap, throwing myself as far as I can against the hot sand until I pull ahead of Melanie. The sun lands hard against me, and sweat streaks down the back of my neck, smelling like sunscreen and salt, but I'm determined to maintain my lead.

We hop around the cones Ms. Barlowe placed a few yards away from the starting line and race our way back. I miscalculate a hop, and the effort sends me flying across the sand. I collide with the ground, a mouthful of sand for my troubles. But no way I'm letting Melanie win. I heave myself back to my feet and compensate for the lost time by throwing myself forward to the finish line, inches before she reaches it.

Done with my part of the race, I collapse onto the ground and wriggle out of the sack so that Liam can take over the next leg. The wet sand beneath me clings to the sweat running down my back, but I don't care. Melanie flops onto the ground next to me, patting my shoulder with a sandy hand.

"You're a worthy opponent," she tells me, breaths heaving.

My returned compliment is interrupted by a particularly large wave, which rushes forward enough to meet our bodies.

I let it rinse the sand off me, relishing in the wave's surprising warmth. As it recedes, I climb to my feet.

"Let's ask about Delos before beach volleyball inevitably puts Ms. Barlowe in a bad mood," I say.

"Does she not like volleyball or something?" Melanie asks as she follows me across the sand.

I eye George and Amalia, who are moments away from physically pushing each other into the water to win. "I just have a feeling the volleyball is going to hit someone in the face at some point."

Putting five thousand dollars and a prestigious prize on the line has brought out the inner academic in all of us. Or at least, the part of academia that's less about nerding out over our field and more about standing out in it—at any cost. As if to prove my point, George collides with the sand, and Amalia hops neatly over him to claim the win.

I swoop over to Ms. Barlowe before she can process the race, and I explain Melanie's idea to her. She nods as she listens, her eyes flicking between the two of us.

"Okay," she says. "I'm going to have to get in touch with your parents and get some permission slip signatures, but that sounds fine as long as Melanie stays with you."

I nod, meeting Melanie's eye. "Definitely."

Melanie cheers. "It's going to be amazing."

It's as she says this, as it becomes too late to change my mind, that the reality sinks in. A whole day away from the cohort, just Melanie and me, island-hopping together.

I can't tell if I'm excited or if I'm scared out of my wits.

CHAPTER TEN

WE EVENTUALLY MAKE IT TO MYKONOS by way of Naxos, leaving early enough in the morning that we dock in time for an early lunch. Delos is a mere hop away from Mykonos, and I'm buzzing with excitement to get there after lunch.

"I've actually never been to Delos before," Melanie says as we roam around the Mykonos port in search of food. Fishing boats and larger vessels alike bob in the clear blue waves by the docks. We're making our way down the paved semicircle curved around the water. The stone-paved walkway is home to taverna awnings stretched out against one another, plush wicker seats set up in their shade, photo-laden menu boards enticing passersby at each entrance.

I snort. "Some guide you're going to be."

She rolls her eyes at me, then links my arm in hers. "We're going to have the best day."

"Thanks for coming with me," I say.

"Of course." Melanie smiles at me. "I'm glad we're friends."

"Me too," I say. Liam's words echo loud in my ears. Am I glad we're friends? Or do I wish we were something else?

The sun reflects off the sea and flashes in my eyes. I blink to clear my vision of light spots. I need to just stay in the moment. That's all. *Stop asking* questions, I beg of my brain. *Just let me be free. Just turn it off, just for this one day.*

We find a little taverna tucked away in one of the many marble-paved side streets and are led to an outdoor table across from a bright bougainvillea plant making its way up the wall opposite. Its vibrant colors pop against the white-washed walls of the buildings that line the street. A stray cat mews as it streaks up the pathway.

Melanie refused to indulge eating anywhere that had a view of the ocean.

"That's just code for *tourist trap where the food is terrible,*" she assures me as we take our seats.

The place she picked is small and largely empty, given that it's relatively early for lunch. What it lacks in human customers, it makes up for in cats. I coo at a gray tabby that slinks its way along the white walls.

"So, what are you thinking for your project?" Melanie asks me after we order.

I squirm in my seat. "What a loaded question."

She laughs. "I get that face. I'm going into junior year, which means I'm officially starting the IB program at my school.

I'm already stressing about what my extended essay is going to be."

"IB?" I ask, glad to get the heat off me for a moment.

"International Baccalaureate," Melanie explains. "It's sort of like AP, with advanced classes and a test, but it's a two-year program, and there are a few other requirements in addition to the classes if you're going for the full program, which I am."

"Like the extended essay?" I ask.

She nods. "You can pick any of your classes to base your project in. I'm doing physics for my science requirement, but I have no idea what I want to do for my essay."

"You have time, though," I assure her. We pause as the waitress returns with our food. We ordered a string of appetizers to share, and I dig into the dolmades as soon as they're dropped onto the table. The soft vine leaves give way to a warm rice filling that provides immediate comfort even in the face of Melanie's question.

"More than you do, that's for sure," Melanie says with a teasing grin. "Which brings me back to my question."

"I have no fresh clue what I'm going to do," I confess. "I've been taking photos, so maybe something with photography? I really have no idea."

Melanie wrinkles her nose. "That's the worst. And the stuff you're all doing is so open-ended."

"I usually love it that way." After a lifetime of rigid academic rules and strict rubrics, the creative freedom and spirit of exploration with which Ms. Barlowe designs our work feels like a breath of air. "But the competition added all this pressure. I feel totally frozen up. And . . ."

I trail off, suddenly self-conscious of how much I've been talking. If I keep going, she's going to know how ceaselessly whiny I am.

"And?" Melanie prompts.

"Well." I clear my throat. "Everyone else in the program is doing *such* cool stuff. I feel like nothing I do can measure up."

Melanie rolls her eyes at this. "I see you're a fellow self-doubter."

"I don't think so," I say with a breathy laugh. "Like, objectively, everyone is doing amazing work, and I still have no idea how to get started."

"But I'm sure that when you find your inspiration, you'll be just as great," Melanie says with a shrug.

I give her a small smile. She says it as though it's a certainty, in a way that makes it hard to doubt her. It's enough to bring a little relief to the endless spiral of my brain, a soft peace I'm not used to feeling. The way she recognizes my emotions while trying to coax me out of them loosens the knot in my chest.

It's almost like she's making me feel like myself while pushing me to grow, some might say.

Not *me*, of course. Just some.

"I'm sure your extended essay will be the same," I tell her, filled with the urge to return the gesture. "I'm sure no one's decided what they're doing yet at this point."

"True," Melanie acknowledges. "I'm just so excited to start."

"Nerd," I tease.

She laughs as she digs into the fried calamari. "You're one to talk. Even at the beach, all you people were buried in your books."

I laugh as I dip a warm slice of pita into the tzatziki. The crisp tang of the cool dip is perfect against the warm doughiness of the pita bread, and I can't help the groan that escapes my lips.

Melanie laughs. "I told you the food would be better here."

"You were right," I say, reaching for another pita. "And the views here aren't bad either."

I mean to draw her attention to the bougainvillea blossoming behind her, another stray cat picturesquely cleaning its paw underneath it, but instead, I find my eyes lingering on hers. She blushes as she takes another bite of her calamari.

Heat draws into my own face, and I find myself grasping at anything to run from the romance I've accidentally infused into the moment.

"Can you believe how dramatic the beach games got yesterday?" I say. Nothing will kill this spark between us faster than acknowledging the mess my cohort is devolving into.

It works. Melanie winces, the blush receding from her cheeks as she takes a sip of water. "I felt so bad. Amalia and George seem to have a lot going on."

I catch her up on the plagiarism scandal, her eyes widening as I fill her in on the details.

"Okay, fair enough," she says when I finish. "That drama sounds tough."

"But then last year was okay," I say. "For them, anyway."

This last part slips out without my entirely meaning to say it. I hope Melanie won't notice, but her eyes catch mine.

"What do you mean?"

"Just that I had a hard time, I guess," I admit. "Everyone already being so established in the group and being so much better than me at the work. I felt like a toddler following the big kids around, trying to fit in."

Melanie grins at the image. "I doubt that's true. You seem like you're right in the mix with them. From the outside, at least. I'd never have guessed you were a newcomer."

"Liam helps with that," I say.

"Not just him." Melanie meets my eyes. "Seems like you're close with Lucy too. And you blend right into the group as a whole. I saw the fire in your eye when we potato-sack-raced."

I laugh. "I run track. I'm not about to lose any races, potato sack or no."

"Fair enough," Melanie says. "I just think you fit in more than you give yourself credit for."

I turn the thought over in my mind. I've felt like an outsider all year. Is that just a story I've been telling myself, a play the brain gremlin is putting on for its own nefarious purposes?

Once we pay for lunch, we head back to the docks to take the ferry to Delos. It feels nice, walking side by side with her. So nice that I start feeling oddly self-conscious of my hand dangling in the space between us. It would be so easy—so natural—to reach out and hold hers.

Instead, I ask, "You said you had a lot of drama last year too, right?"

Melanie shudders. "My whole friend group imploded."

"Oh god." I wince sympathetically. "What happened? I mean, only if you want to talk about—"

"Yeah, for sure," Melanie says. "Thanks for asking, honestly. My friends are sick of hearing about it, but I'm still feeling so stuck on it, you know?"

Do I ever. "I was actually crowned Queen of Being Stuck on Things recently, so I know exactly what you mean."

Melanie drops into a curtsy. "An honor to be in your presence, Your Majesty."

I laugh. "The only proper way to honor the title is to talk mad shit."

"Perfect," Melanie says with a laugh. "Basically, I'm in the theater club at my school, and there was cast list drama that blew up in everyone's face. I got a part this other girl wanted, and because she was a senior last year and I was a sophomore, people said I should've quit the play so she could step into the role."

"Huh?" I ask. "Granted, I've never been in theater, but that doesn't . . . sound right."

"I mean, I agree," Melanie says, throwing her hands up. "But it got so bad that I actually started doubting whether I should do it or not. She was really upset. And people were saying that since it was just my second year and her last, she should get priority."

"Isn't that ultimately the teacher's call, though?" I point out.

"You'd think," Melanie mutters. "But people decided that I got the part because my mom works at the school and is good friends with the drama teacher. So they decreed that I was a nepo baby and that the right thing to do was to step down so that Kyra could have the part that was rightfully hers."

"Kyra sounds evil," I say.

"She definitely made last year hard," Melanie says. "I ended up dropping out of the play because rehearsals got so hostile."

I wince, remembering what she told me about her anxiety and how much she hides of herself to please those around her.

"I'm so sorry," I tell her. "You definitely didn't deserve that garbage. Sounds like Kyra's insecurities ended up all over you somehow."

Melanie bridges the air between us to squeeze my hand with hers. I secretly hope she'll never let go, but she drops her fingers after a moment. "Who knew high school could be so dramatic?"

"It should come with a warning label," I agree. I was so ready to leave this all behind in middle school. Although, based on how my dad's book club went this year, I'm starting to worry that drama never stops haunting us.

"But we made it through," Melanie says. "That's gotta be worth something."

"I'm proud of us," I agree.

We make our way to the ferry. It's a little one, with the ride lasting only thirty minutes. I quickly learn that smaller boats only mean more seasickness. The waves hurl us around the sea (lightly rock us in our seats), and every motion sends a sickening jolt through my stomach. Melanie spends the half hour sympathetically patting my back while I bravely limit my complaints to only one a minute.

It's a relief to get onto the sweet, dry land of Delos. Where I might stay forever. Because I'm certainly never getting on a ferry again.

"So, what's your coming-out story?" Melanie asks me as we get off the ferry. It's dry, not just in the "we're not on water anymore" sense but in the literal brown tinges of the tallgrass that sways in the slow, sea-salted breeze.

It's a classic lesbian first-date question.

Not that this is our first date.

I mean. Oh my god. Not that this is a date at all.

"Pretty straightforward," I say with a shrug. "My parents have always been supercool about it. I don't think they were particularly surprised. I talked a *lot* about how pretty Keira Knightley was after seeing Pirates of the Caribbean."

Melanie laughs. "That's an incredible lesbian awakening."

"Thank you," I say, taking a little bow. "Yours was that guy, right?"

"Embarrassingly, it did take dating that boy for me to realize that they are simply not for me," Melanie says. "My parents were fine, but I think my grandma might never get over not planning my and Dimos's wedding. She definitely had a whole secret floral arrangement picked out."

"Maybe she can use them for my sister, get both of them off our backs," I suggest, and Melanie laughs.

We make it off the dock and onto the main stretch of beach. The whole island of Delos is an archaeological site dedicated to the remains of its ancient history. No one lives here, and we have to tour entirely on foot.

I love it already.

We pause to reapply sunscreen. The midday sun is beating down on us, and the archaeological sites where we're going to spend the day visiting offer no shade. Brown grass crunches underfoot as we make our way up the path. Little lizards dart across ahead of us, scrabbling to find shade among the small rocks strewn around the grass. Melanie follows up her reapplication with an incredibly dorky straw hat that I find unbearably endearing.

"Okay, that's adorable," I say.

She tips the edge of the hat at me, and the whole thing bounces. "Sun safety is always sexy. Keep this front of mind."

I laugh as I follow her toward the Theater Quarter, where we examine the remains of what were undoubtedly the fanciest houses on the island back when it was populated. Still unsure about where I'm going with my project, I stop to photograph everything, from the details of the slate slabs paving the narrow streets to the pillars framing the courtyards in some of the homes.

"Sorry," I tell Melanie as I pause to take yet another series of photos, this one documenting the details of a bright blue mosaic floor. "I know this can't be the most exciting thing for you."

"Please don't apologize," Melanie says, brushing me off. "First of all, we're literally here for your project. And secondly, I can't imagine anything cuter than watching you be all absorbed in your work like this."

I duck my face behind my phone so she can't see my blush. "I don't know. Have you seen you in that hat?"

When I stand and fall into step beside her, I let our fingers intertwine. Both of our palms are sweaty from the relentlessness of the sun, but I don't mind. Her skin warms mine in a pleasant way that's different from the heat of the day.

We linger awhile at the House of Dionysus before heading over to the Theater of Delos. It's an impressive amphitheater that could seat upwards of five thousand spectators. The ancient stone seats curve in a semicircle around the stage. The rows are worn from years of serving the audience of the theater and from the winds drifting across the space. Theaters are quickly becoming my favorite sites to visit. The idea that people have been telling one another stories for this long always gets me choked up.

"Do you think they had cast list drama in 200 BCE?" I ask Melanie, and she snorts.

"There's a Kyra in every theater," she assures me.

We pass through the Terrace of the Lions. It's a continuation of the paved path we've been following but with impressive stone-carved lions roaring over us from their pedestals. They seem stuck out of place, standing proudly amid these tall-grasses and a few lean trees.

We end our tour with the Sanctuary of Apollo, which is now largely in ruins, save for four columns standing watch over the space where the temple once stood. Apollo was Artemis's twin brother, born on this island to hide their mother from Hera's jealous rage after Zeus fathered them.

Classic Zeus.

When we finish with the outdoor sites, we reach the museum. Slipping through its glass and into the cool interior is a relief. Melanie walks me through the exhibit, doing her best impression of a tour guide to make up for her lack of knowledge of the island as a whole.

"And here we have another broken statue," Melanie says when we pause in front of a marble bust. "It's very old. Please take notes."

I giggle my way through the museum, though my laughter dies in my throat when I realize it's time to get back on the ferry of death and doom.

We're supposed to head straight home and have dinner on the ferry ride to Naxos, but, as Melanie points out when we finally get back onto the steady land of Mykonos, where's the fun in that?

"Whereas the fun in Mykonos," she says, "is incredibly easy to find. I'll just tell my mom we missed the ferry. It'll be fine."

My inherent fear of getting in trouble spikes for a moment, but it's quickly quelled by the sounds of Mykonos nightlife picking up around us. Lively chatter fills the streets as dinnertime packs the tavernas, and music floats in the air as the nightclubs come to life. It's easy to nod my head and follow Melanie to dinner.

The taverna bustles with activity—and, more importantly, with cats—and we agree to split as many dishes as we can.

"What's your dream life?" Melanie asks me after we order.

I laugh at the broadness of her question, and she raises her eyebrows at me sternly.

"I'd love to travel, spend my life researching. Working an elusive position in academia that pays all the bills and won't suck my soul out," I say. She nods, her big brown eyes staring deep into mine, and I find myself blurting out more without thinking. "And I guess . . . in my dream life, I'm not so trapped in my head all the time. I can be free, sometimes, of the constant worrying. Not waste so much of my life proving to myself over and over again that everything's okay. Maybe even believe it."

I'm not sure I've ever admitted that to anyone before. Not even Liam. I've complained to him about Paige since my parents made me start going to see her, but I haven't admitted that sometimes the way she talks about obsessive thought patterns sounds like she's been inside my brain, sees what happens there.

"That sounds like it sucks," Melanie says softly. "I'm sorry you deal with that."

"Thanks," I murmur. "What's your dream life like, then?"

"Free too," Melanie says. "Of all the expectations, you

know? I guess maybe not free of other people's expectations existing, because that's out of my control entirely, but free of caring about them so much. They weigh on me so heavily now."

"I get that," I say. I know what it's like to carry mental weight everywhere you go. "It must be exhausting."

Melanie nods, and for a moment, I can see the tiredness flash in her eyes. She reaches across the table and squeezes my hand, a now-familiar gesture that makes me smile.

"Well, here's to our dream lives, then," she says. I meet her eyes across the table, and it's easy to smile back. Easy to think that, just maybe, it's all within reach.

After dinner it should be easy to get on the ferry and go back to Naxos. Not just easy but increasingly urgent.

But the sun is setting, and we can hear the waves crashing against the sandy shores of the beach, and who are we to ignore the undeniable call of the evening?

So we miss the next ferry, giggling as we make our way down to the beach. It's golden at this hour, the sinking sun casting a pale pink glow on the slow-moving water and the quickly cooling sand. The beauty of the earth comes alive under the setting rays, the pale colors of the day's last light softening the edges of the world. I sink into an ease, letting the harsh light of day melt into the cool, whispering twilight air.

This time it's my hand that reaches for hers, and by the

time we've reached the sandy expanse of the beach, our fingers are intertwined. I can feel her heartbeat drumming in her fingertips, racing against my skin. It creates an electric tingle between us, one that makes me afraid of meeting her eye. Deepening the connection that's already simmering between us feels akin to throwing myself off a cliff without knowing what awaits at the bottom.

Besides, the sunset draws both our eyes to the horizon. We watch the sinking of the light in silence, our hands saying everything they need to.

Of course, my brain is coming up with a *lot* more to say. My heartbeat thrums under the weight of the warnings pressing against my skull. *You should be running away from this moment. What are you doing? Why are you here? The ferry left, and now you're stranded here, and everything is about to be ruined, and there's nothing you can do about it.* A headache blossoms at my temples.

I try to refocus on the moment, blinking as the first stars of the night emerge. They dot the inky twilight. The first shimmer of the rising full moon hovers over the horizon opposite the just-sunken sun.

"What are you thinking about?" Melanie asks me, probably unaware of what a loaded question she's asked.

"Just . . ." I pause, taking in the sky. "How beautiful tonight is."

Probably a safer bet than admitting what's actually flashing through my brain right now.

I'm right. Melanie's face lights up.

"It really is," she agrees. "I'm glad I got to spend today with you. Just the two of us."

She adds this last part shyly, like she's not sure about saying it out loud. It makes me realize fully, for the first time, what I've been putting her through this summer. Taking two steps forward only to run away from her as soon as this thing between us starts to feel too real—only to show back up the next day as if nothing happened.

It's no wonder she chose to run away herself that night on the boat.

I'm hit with a rush of gratitude for her, for this night, for the full moon that's slowly rising above the sea and hitting everything with its shimmering silver light.

Melanie herself shines, and I can't quite tell if the shining is coming from the moon or from within her. Or maybe it's coming from me, and I'm finally seeing things clearly.

"I'm glad you're here," I tell her.

And I'm the one who leans in first.

Our lips meet, and the softness of her undoes me. The world around us silences until it's only the two of us left standing here. Her hand slides across my lower back, pulling me closer. Which is exactly where I want to be.

Her smile when we break apart carries the light of all the stars above us.

"I thought that would never happen," she admits. We're still close enough that my nose brushes against hers as I laugh.

"I'm glad it did," I whisper.

When we kiss again, it feels like the most natural thing in the world. Like we should've been doing this the entire time. I want to kick myself for how much of it I've wasted.

But then she tilts toward me again, my fingers twining into her hair as I pull her closer to meet the softness of her lips with mine. Her touch is enough to ease my worries about the time we've lost.

And it's okay. We have a moonlit beach walk and an entire ferry ride back to make up for it.

PAIGE: Hi Natalie! I hope you're having the best time in Greece. Just a reminder that I'm always here if you need a check-in at any point.

PAIGE: Hi Natalie! Sorry to bother you on what I'm sure is the summer of a lifetime. Your parents wanted me to check in and see if you have any time this week to schedule a session. I can work with the time difference, just let me know!

NATALIE: hi so sorry for the late response! I'm all good but thank you

PAIGE: No worries! Just let me know if that changes. I'm here if you need me!

CHAPTER ELEVEN

THE SUNLIGHT STREAMING INTO MY ROOM splashes harshly on every single one of my mistakes. I squint in the morning light, but even without my looking directly at what it's illuminating, my brain flashes loud sirens across all the memories of the past couple of days. I can't ignore what the hard reality of morning brings.

Ditching Liam *again* to do yet another bucket list item with Melanie instead of him.

Opening up to her, letting her in on all the scariest parts of me.

Kissing her on the beach.

Spending the ferry ride home alternating between making out and looking at the stars. My head on her shoulder. Her hand in mine. Entwined like we belong together.

As if I could ever belong with anyone. I'm just not meant

for romance. That's for people like my parents, with their gooey date nights, or for Lizzie, with her dreamy wedding. People who are willing to give up huge parts of themselves to let the idea of love take them over. I haven't even gotten up yet, and the weight of last night's mistakes threaten to never let me get up again.

I strain against them with everything I have to make it to the shower. I have no idea how to get through the day.

Turns out, the secret to getting through it is to pretend I'm so immersed in my project that I simply cannot come up for air. Not when Melanie tries to find me at breakfast.

The worst part is, Liam does the same. I can't tell if he's actually busy with his work or if he's angry at me, and I don't dare ask. I'm afraid I already know the answer.

The second worst part is that I'm not making any real progress on my project at all. My brain is too caught up in what's been going on to focus on the page in front of me. My fingers tremble when I try to write. The letters blur when I try to focus on my reading. My pounding brain drowns out any relief the washing sounds of the waves might bring.

It's a relief when our time in Paros comes to an end. Our next stop is Corinth, which means a day of being on a ferry and a bus. As soon as we get onto the ferry, I tuck myself into a corner of the boat and flop my still-empty notebook open across my lap. Clicking my pen like I might have something to add at any moment, I stare at the blank page that's become my constant companion.

We're back to cutting through the clarity of the seawater, the ferry frothing waves in our wake. There's not a cloud above us. We're surrounded by a perfect blue orb, the lightest shades of midday teal stretching forever in every direction. But instead of rocking me into the peace that I've felt these past few days, the color makes me feel trapped. Like I'm entombed in a steadfast bubble I'll never be able to pop.

A loud burst of laughter tears my eyes away from the page. I glance up to see Liam and Lucy giggling over paper cups of coffee. Liam's eyes wander across the deck and meet mine, but he quickly shifts his gaze back to Lucy to laugh at her next joke.

My heart might as well rip out of my chest and flop on the spiral of my notebook like a fish on the dry deck of a boat. *He just flicked his eyes away*, I try to tell myself, but it's so much more than that. With not even a smile to throw my way, let alone an invitation to join them—could it be clearer that all my worst fears are true? He's mad at me. I've finally driven him away too. Just like I have with everyone else.

"Can I join you?" Melanie's shadow falls across my lap.

I look at her. The sun lights up her hair from behind, making its frizzy ends blaze against the deep blue of the sky. She looks beautiful. Blinking, I force myself to look away, back down at my knees.

"I— Yes." Choking that out feels like a feat of strength

not even Hercules could tackle. My vocal cords constrict on themselves under the pressure of Liam not looking my way again. Everything feels like it's spiraling completely out of my reach, and I can't tell where to grab hold of it to try to fix things.

She settles, cross-legged, on the wood deck next to me, leaning against the whitewashed railing of the ferry. It's only when I lift my hand to brush my hair out of my face that I realize Melanie has wrapped her fingers in mine. She brings her hand back into her lap, tugging at the ends of her shirt.

"Sorry," I say. "I didn't mean— I just. Um."

"You okay?" Melanie asks.

I nod. "Yeah. Sorry. I'm fine."

"I had such a good time last night," Melanie says, her fingers drifting back to my hand. The warmth of her used to calm me, but now that I've let myself fall headfirst into undeniably romantic territory, it just sends prickles of caution up my skin.

"Me too," I say, because it's true. Last night was lovely. It's this morning that sucks.

"I was thinking we could try to sneak off tonight," Melanie says, looking down at our entwined hands. "There are a few places in Corinth I'd love to show you."

I have no idea how to respond. The thought of another night alone with her is laced with both temptation and dread. I'm caught between the urges to run forward and away, and I end up frozen between her sentences.

"We don't have that much time left before you head back," Melanie says softly. "I want to make the most of it."

She means well; I can tell. Her eyes are lit up with the hope behind her words. I can't stand to crush it.

But at the same time, I flinch away from what she's saying. I have so little time left of this trip and everything I wanted to make of it—not romance but time with Liam, who's now further away than ever. Not falling in love but time with my project, which is still nothing more than a blank page. She's staked a claim on time that was never hers to have, and my every instinct screams for me to defend it.

"I just . . . Honestly, there's just so much going on with the trip and the project and everything. I really loved the other day, and I've loved . . ." I trail off, not sure how to properly explain how I feel. When I think about last night, the bubble in which the two of us spent our day, of course I loved every second. It's the time since then that's been hell. "I just . . . I think I need a little space?"

I cringe at the sound of my own words coming out of my mouth, knowing how they'll be received. I've disappointed her, and the clarity of that hits me as soon as the words fall from my lips. Melanie leans away from me, her wounded eyes scanning my face as if trying to read past my words.

"Not, like, *space* space," I say quickly when I register the hurt in her eyes. "I just mean I feel like I can't be all in right now, but that doesn't mean I don't want to be in at all. Does that make sense?"

It sounds awful. But with Liam not even looking in my direction, with my project nonexistent, what else can I do?

Melanie scrunches her nose. "Yeah, it makes sense. Sorry. I didn't mean to—"

"You didn't," I say quickly, desperate to ease the hurt hunching her shoulders. "I just . . . want to be clear about where I'm at."

Though I'm not sure *clear* is what I'm being at all. Translating the scramble from thought to speech is impossible to begin with. I have no idea how to do it well.

The resulting hurt is written all over Melanie's face. My heartbeat flaps uselessly in my stomach, pumping acid instead of blood through my veins. Before I can stop myself, I reach out and take her hand back. She gives me a small smile in return.

"Sorry," I say. "I don't mean to make this a big thing. I just run anxious."

"So we're good?" she asks.

I nod. "Definitely."

I'm not sure if it's true, but it's all I know to say in this moment. Her hand is warm against mine, and my head won't stop buzzing. I don't know how to make sense of both these truths at the same time. But the buzzing has to be a sign, right? If I were to meet someone who was right for me, I wouldn't feel this anxious around them.

Right?

"Well, I can leave you to your work," Melanie says. She pauses, her eyes lingering on mine, and I wonder if she's hoping that I'll stop her, ask her to stay. I let her down, as I'm becoming so good at doing, by letting her walk away.

When she's rounded the corner and out of sight, regret

pours over me. Last night was one of the most magical nights of my life. Why would I turn down a chance at another? Why can't I let myself be open, like Liam's always saying I should?

But thinking of Liam reminds me why I have to walk away from Melanie.

He's the priority here. Our friendship matters more than anything. If I'm going to ask for space from Melanie, I might as well use it for good. Besides, I have to check to know if he's mad at me or not.

Heart hammering, I force myself off the ground and toward the table Liam and Lucy have claimed.

"How's the project going?" Liam asks when I reach their table. I meet his eye, trying to read what's there. Is there something off in his tone?

"Oh, you know," I say, keeping my voice light enough to float on the water. "Penning a masterpiece, as per usual."

"I don't doubt it," Liam says. The upward quirk of his lips sends a shot of relief through my exhausted veins. His smile is familiar and warm, a sure sign that we're okay.

But then it slides off his face as he turns back to Lucy. "Mine is feeling like trash right now."

"I'm sure it's amazing," I say reflexively. His work is always amazing, yet he loves to be his own harshest critic. His only critic, some would say.

He's still looking to Lucy, though, which sends a new wave of anxious fluttering through my stomach. Does he wish I would leave? Why would he rather turn to Lucy with this than me?

"Nat's right," Lucy says. "Your stuff is always amazing."

Liam rubs the back of his neck. "I don't know. I feel like I've hit a wall. Will you . . . ?"

He pushes his notebook to the middle of the table. Lucy snatches it up before I can so much as crane my neck over to read it. She reads it quickly before passing the notebook to me.

"It's gorgeous," she says as I read.

"Seriously," I say, jumping in before I'm fully done, scared of losing my foothold in their conversation. "You're amazing at this." I pointedly tap the final line of the poem, tilting the notebook so he can see. He rolls his eyes, but the quirk is back in the corners of his lips.

"Yeah, okay, that part is literary genius," he agrees. The relief is back in my chest, so easily dispelling the acid with just the knowledge that he's feeling better—and that I'm the one who helped him.

I hate how easy it is to quell this feeling. All it takes is one shot of reassurance to calm the storm that rages in my chest. Because I know it's always temporary. Relief forever is impossible.

Still, I'll take it while I can get it. I swallow a deep breath of the sea-salted air, letting the smell of the waves rush into my newly loosened lungs, and spend the rest of the ferry ride laughing over pretzel chips with Liam and Lucy.

Nothing hits better than the tightly tucked-in sheets of a hotel-room bed after a day of endless travel. We ferried to

Athens and bused from there to Corinth, the entirety of the Greek countryside flashing by the dirty windows of our bus. The day is a blur of seawater and dry hills and spiky green trees, the blue dome of the sky always clear above us.

My limbs are relishing the space to spread out and the softness of the bedspread. I answer the FaceTime from my family group chat without sitting up, the pillow smushing against the right side of my face.

"How's Greece?" Mom coos as soon as her face fills my screen.

I roll over onto my back, lifting the phone above my face. "It's gorgeous. I'm learning so much."

"I can't believe there's more to learn," Dad yells from the kitchen, where I can see him prepping pasta sauce in the background. I know the kitchen must smell amazing, and it makes me ache for home.

"There's always more to learn," I holler back at him. Mom gives me a proud smile, and it floods me with relief. It's been so long since I've actually been able to talk to my parents, and I need the reminder that they care about me, in addition to Lizzie's wedding, more than I realized.

"Your itinerary says you're in Crete," Mom says, squinting at her computer.

"Corinth," I correct.

Mom sighs as she scrolls a little further. "Is it the last week of July already? We're so behind on wedding preparations."

I don't answer, because, well, what is there to say?

"Have you been in touch with Paige?" Mom asks.

I shake my head. "I'm having such a good time, I haven't needed to."

Mom purses her lips. "That's not how therapy is supposed to work, Natalie. Paige says that it's important to—"

"Mom," I snap. "I'm in *Greece*. Can't I just enjoy it?"

"Tell me about it so far, then," Mom says, though I can see in her eyes her plans to keep pushing the issue.

I give her the rundown of everything that's happened over the past few days. Well, everything academic, that is. I leave out the awkwardness between Liam and me, the weird tension simmering throughout the cohort, and certainly any hint of kissing. The last thing I need is for my "high school sweetheart" parents to get wind of the mere suggestion of romance. They glom on to the possibility of love faster than anything. As if it's the most important thing I could have.

"And tomorrow we're visiting the archaeological museum and the Temple of Apollo," I say.

"That sounds lovely," Mom says. "We're very busy here too. Remember, the rehearsal is scheduled for the week after you get back, so you'll need to be ready."

"Of course," I say, propping myself up on the mattress. "I've thought of nothing else."

"Don't get an attitude," Mom says. "It's a big day."

"I don't have an attitude," I argue, even though I objectively do. I can feel a waspishness seeping into my tone that I can't seem to control. But what am I supposed to do here? Dedicate my every waking thought to preparing for Lizzie's wedding while I'm literally thousands of miles away?

Mom gives me a stern look through the camera, and I force myself to take a deep breath. "I'll be ready for the wedding, Mom. Promise."

"Thank you," she says, softening. "Now, I really think you should talk to Paige about—"

"I have to go," I say. "It's getting late here."

"Okay," Mom says, "but please think about it."

"I will," I mutter, having no intention of doing so.

My mom hangs up the phone as Liam comes back into the room. The hotel has an indoor pool, and he brings its chlorine scent back with him.

"How are the parents?" he asks.

I roll my eyes. "Matrimonially obsessed."

"My parents are so excited," Liam tells me as he shakes the water out of his curls, spraying droplets on the floor around him. "They got me and my dad matching pocket squares for the occasion."

I giggle. "Can't wait to see that."

"Do you wanna talk about it?" he asks.

"Talk about what?"

He gives me a look, and I glance at the now-darkened phone screen my mom just vacated.

"No, it's okay," I say. The truth is, I don't want to bother him with any more of my nonsense. It's not going to help our friendship if I'm always whining about my problems. "Thanks, though."

He nods and disappears into the bathroom. I flop down onto the bed, wondering how I let myself get to this point.

Other people seem to manage just fine. Friends, a girlfriend, normal relationships with their family. All I seem to attract is unspoken tension no one knows how to name.

It occurs to me that I could ask Paige. She did say I could reach out to her *at any point* during my trip. But it's probably outside her working hours by now. Besides, she'd just tell me that I have to breathe through the moment or something, probably.

Seems safest to just go to bed.

CHAPTER TWELVE

THE WORST PART ABOUT ALL THIS drama is that it has me seriously out of shape. All the morning activities on the itinerary have replaced my early-morning running habit, and I refuse to allow my second-place classmate Sarah Muller to beat me out when we get back onto the track at the start of next year.

Besides, running has always been the best—the only—way to clear my head. The music blasting through my headphones drowns out any other sound, and all I can focus on is my sneaker soles hitting the pavement. I steer myself uphill, hoping to end up with a nice view of the ocean. It's still dark out, but dawn is hinting on the horizon well enough that I can see the path in front of me.

I wish I could say the same for the day.

There's a text from Melanie sitting in my phone, one I have no idea how to respond to.

Good night! Can we hang tomorrow? xx

It's a perfectly reasonable text. I want to answer with a wholehearted *Yes, of course!* She makes me laugh, makes me forget how far I am from home. It's the easiest yes.

Or at least it should be, but the thought of it is enough to send me back into a spiral that not even running can fend off all the way. Because what if Liam gets even angrier with me? What if Lucy notices, and the whole cohort starts taunting me about dating again?

Wading through this mess, even if it's just to answer a text, feels impossible. I'm completely locked in my own head. All I can do is keep running, oxygen slamming into my lungs with every breath, until I make it to the top of this hill. I focus on the dirt that stirs between my footsteps, the lizards ducking under rocks as I pass, the call of a bird in the trees overhead. My lungs heave in the freshness of the clean air, carrying the scent of summer leaves and sunshine even this early in the morning.

At least I was right. I do get a good view of the ocean through the trees, the water just beginning to sparkle under the rising sun.

In that moment, it feels so clear. I can see all the way down to the shimmering waves, and I watch them crash against the beach, my pulse thudding hard from the uphill run. But not everything in my life has to feel like an uphill run. Maybe

I can let some things just happen. I've told Melanie I don't want us to turn into anything serious or all-consuming. What harm can one more night together do?

I text back, *Yes*.

The Temple of Apollo in Corinth is one of the earliest-known Doric temples in the Greek mainland.

This is all I have written in my notebook, and I knew this before I showed up. But the vibes are distinctly weird today. Melanie's taken off from the tour to visit some cousins, and the cohort has stopped all pretense of getting along. Amalia and George stay pointedly on opposite sides of any space we enter, Henry flitting awkwardly between the two like a confused puppy. Lucy sticks by Amalia, while Liam and I hover in the entryway, unsure where to go next.

The midday sun beats down on us, the ruins offering no hint of shade. Everything about how we're acting is illuminated in the harshest noon light.

"This is exactly what it felt like last year," Liam mutters. "Except this time nothing's really happened."

I think back to Amalia and George's first argument that day in Athens. It feels like so long ago, their bickering clouding over our visit to Monastiraki. Lucy was so committed to group-togetherness then, and now her arm is looped protectively around Amalia's as they examine one of the columns with overly close attention. Bodhi stands by them with his arms crossed, nodding along to everything they say. Even Henry, who mastered the art of the go-between last year, is starting to linger longer at George's side.

Liam and I pretend not to notice.

"We should do something," I tell him as we make it around to another side of the temple. It's a rectangular structure; many of its columns remain, but little else still stands. "This trip wasn't supposed to destroy us."

"What's really being destroyed, though?" Liam mutters. "It was like this last year."

"And you worked through it," I remind him. "You can do that again. I don't think we should write people off completely for a mistake."

"But is this a mistake or a pattern?" Liam points out.

This forces me to fall silent as I mull over the wisdom in his words. I pause under the rare shade cast by one of the columns, and I stare off to the rocky mountain looming in the distance. Between us lies a long stretch of dried grass, patches of trees shooting up toward the watchful sky. He's right, of course. Forgiving a friend for a mistake is one thing, but looking past the same mistake over and over again is a different story.

So where does that leave me? Because in spite of all my best efforts, I always seem to end up trying to claw myself out of the same hole, the same spiral pulling me ever downward. I feel utterly trapped in this pattern. But Liam doesn't have to be.

"Are you mad at me?" I ask him quietly.

He puts an arm around my shoulders. "Of course not. Why would I be?"

I can think of many reasons, and they're all numbered in the bucket list still scribbled in his notebook. We haven't done a single item on it together, but I've already checked most of them off.

Now could be the time to tell him. To confess everything and apologize. But then his hand would fall from my shoulder, and I'd be alone forever, and everything I've sacrificed to keep our friendship alive would have been for nothing.

I can't bring myself to do it. I'm an awful friend. Trapped, still, in the same pattern.

Melanie texts me as soon as she's back at the hotel, and I bounce down to the lobby to meet her as fast as I can. I'm determined to break at least one pattern today. Fleeing from her can be the one, though the feeling I had on my run this morning feels harder to grasp on to after the simmering tension of the day. I want to find a way to make this work. All of it—love in all its forms, the way so many people seem to manage it without any of the difficulties I create for myself in its path.

When I see Melanie, I break out into an easy grin.

"Sorry I've been so weird lately," I tell her as she loops her arm around mine.

"As long as we're okay," Melanie says softly.

I nod. "Of course we are."

We walk through the hotel doors and into the cool night

air. There's no particular destination in mind, but aimlessly wandering the streets on a warm summer evening with her hand in mine sounds like a destination enough.

"I was a little thrown," Melanie admits. "I wasn't sure what prompted you to feel that way."

"It's not you," I tell her quickly.

"'It's me'?" Melanie quips.

"It sounds hokey, but it's true," I insist. "At the very least, it's my . . ." I'm not sure how much I want to admit. I've already told her some things, but I haven't even told Liam that Paige has me formally diagnosed. The label isn't something I've wanted to advertise to anyone.

But I want Melanie to understand me, I realize.

"I was diagnosed with OCD this year," I tell Melanie at last. "It hasn't been easy to process. I think it's sort of helping me understand how my brain works, but it's also making me completely rethink everything I thought I knew about myself."

In the moments when I'm willing to admit that Paige is probably right, I can make sense of the patterns that drag my thoughts down and tank my emotions with them. I just still have no idea how to claw my way out of the hole these patterns have dug for me.

"Whoa," Melanie says. "That sounds hard."

"So I guess I'm just . . . skittish about new romance," I say quietly. The soft night air rustles around us, almost swallowing my words.

There's more I could say. I know that. I could tell her about what it feels like when I think about falling in love—like the steel jaws of a trap are closing around me. I could confess that, no matter how much I love the time we spend together, there's always a part of me that's crouched at the starting line, poised to run at any moment. That I have no idea how to turn that part off. Or if I even should, if that part is protecting me.

I know what Liam and Lucy would say about it. Maybe that's why I haven't told them. I certainly know how it would make Melanie feel.

So I keep my mouth shut.

"I don't mind taking things slow," Melanie tells me. "I just want to be clear on where we stand."

"Of course," I say. "I should've just been up-front about how I've been feeling."

"It's a hard thing to talk about," Melanie says. "Thank you for telling me."

I answer her with a kiss, and we spend the rest of the evening much better occupied.

CHAPTER THIRTEEN

I FLIP THROUGH THE PHOTOS I'VE taken so far on the trip as the bus rumbles its way toward Nafplio. This summer has transformed my camera roll into a blur of vibrant blues and purples, of white columns standing straight against the brightness of the sky, of enough orange stray cats to win that part of the scavenger hunt twice over, of the crisp white-washed houses of the islands and the animated street art of the city. I've documented so much on this trip, but I have no idea how to translate the awe I felt at all these sites into anything meaningful.

Liam plops down onto the seat next to me, and I look up at him in surprise. He's usually too carsick to be anywhere near the back of the bus, but I couldn't handle sitting too near the rest of the cohort for this ride.

"I can't take it anymore," he mutters. "I'd rather vom than listen to Amalia make one more pointed comment."

I shudder. "Oof. Is it really that bad up there?"

"I have no idea what they're even arguing about," Liam says, shaking his head.

"Does she still think he's trying to steal her project idea?" I ask, tilting my head to watch Amalia and George stare out opposite windows in pointed silence.

"That's what I heard her saying, but it feels like there's gotta be more to it," Liam says under his breath.

I sigh, rubbing the back of my neck. The truth is, there's more to what's going on between Liam and me as well. The abandoned bucket list, the awkward silences, the certainty that he's simmering with unspoken fury. But I'm too nervous to bring any of it up.

The bus takes a sharp, veering turn, bringing our first sight of Nafplio into view. The vibrancy of its colors makes it feel like I'm looking at a photo with the saturation turned way up. The jasmine and bougainvillea explode in rich purples and sweet whites among picturesque streets cutting through the red-tiled roofs of the buildings. Beyond the leafy greenery outlining the city lies another view of the sea, the noon sun's rays scattering across its surface. At the bus's sudden movement, the edges of Liam's face go pale.

"I hate the back of the bus," he says, and I pat his shoulder.

Besides, now clearly isn't the time to have this conversation.

"I believe in you," I tell him.

"Can't believe I might vom anyway," he mutters, and I laugh a little too loudly, trying to convince both of us that things are okay.

We spend our first morning in Nafplio at Bourtzi Castle, a Venetian tower on a little island a short ride away from the mainland. I sit next to Liam on the boat and tell myself that this counts as respecting our bucket list.

I do not believe this, to be clear.

But as soon as I plop down in the row next to him, I glance over at Melanie, and a fresh stab of guilt spears through me like a hot knife. Should I be sitting next to her? Is it a trick of the light, or is that hurt dashing her eyes?

The thought is enough to make me want to fling myself into the water and swim home. The water's dazzlingly clear enough that I'm tempted into thinking I could make it. I'll never tire of watching a boat cut through the water, sending frothy wavelets to either side of our path. It would be so easy to just swim back to shore.

Instead, I lean on Liam's shoulder, and he tilts to rest his cheek against the top of my head. The boat rocks us gently enough that I don't get seasick. We reach the island a few minutes later. It's a small plot of paved land, the round stone structure of the castle emerging from one end, a fortress watching over the sea. As we climb from the rocking boat onto the steady dock, I scoot over to find Melanie.

"How was your breakfast?" I ask her. "Can't believe there was no morning baklava here."

She grins. "You know that's not a thing, right?"

"I'm on a mission to make it one."

"You know what?" she says, slipping her hand in mine. "I support you."

"Thanks," I say solemnly. My palm immediately breaks out into a cold sweat, almost as if my body is trying to repel her. Is that a thing? Should I be paying attention to these signs?

I'm itching to take my phone out and look this up, but I can hardly do that in front of Melanie, so instead I look out at the water shimmering around the castle, the hard near-noon sunlight turning everything into the kind of brilliant gold you can't look right at. Bright white spots dance in my vision as I turn back to Melanie, and I can't quite see her face. All the same, I let her guide me around the pavement to the rounded edge of the castle. The sun beats down on us, and I dab at the sweat accumulating on the back of my neck with my free hand.

"I should find Liam," I say when we reach the castle's chapel. She looks surprised, so I add, "He loves a fresco."

"Who doesn't," she says, her tone flattening.

My footsteps seem to echo loudly across the dim interior of the chapel as I cross it to find Liam, alerting everyone with my movements. He smiles at me when I reach him.

"Don't act like you and Melanie weren't just holding hands," he says, smirking.

I feel the steep red flooding my cheeks. In my haste to make sure Melanie and I were okay, I didn't pause to think about the fact that other people were watching. Now everyone knows, and I've just gifted them all something to talk about. Everyone is yearning for a break from Amalia and George's drama, so this new gossip train might never run out of steam.

"Friends can hold hands," I remind him, squeezing his fingers to prove my point.

He rolls his eyes as he turns back to the frescoes. "Not friends who are also clearly attracted to each other. Why are you trying to hide this from me?"

His voice cracks a bit as he reaches the word *me*, and I realize that the secrets are only adding to how mad he is at me.

"I'm sorry," I say quickly, my voice lowering as Lucy wanders past with Bodhi. "I'm not trying to hide anything from *you*. I just . . ."

"But I'm the only one here," Liam whispers.

I nod, swallowing hard to keep the tears from spiking past the corners of my eyes. His frustration feels like it's pressing against the insides of my skull, and I have to swallow hard to push past the thick lump of anxiety balling in my throat. Right now has to be about Liam. It's just that the thing about anxiety is that sometimes it feels inherently selfish, like it's always dragging my gaze inward so that I'm processing everything through the lens of my own self-consciousness, contorting it to fit the box of whatever I'm worrying about that day.

I take a deep breath, the kind that (and I do hate to admit it) Paige taught me about.

"I'm sorry," I repeat, my voice steady this time. "Trust me,

I can feel myself being weird about all of this. I just feel so trapped in it. I'm sorry it hurt your feelings."

Liam nudges my shoulder with his. "It's okay. It's not about me. I'm just worried about you, I guess."

"Sorry I'm fundamentally broken," I quip, wiggling my fingers at him.

He rolls his eyes but gives me a pity laugh. "You're not broken."

It feels like I am. Romance comes so *easily* to everyone around me. My parents love reminiscing about when they first started dating in high school, and it always felt like they watched our first relationships with the expectation that things would work out just as easily for us. And of course, now that Lizzie's ready to meet her freshman-year-of-college boyfriend at the end of the aisle, and Andrea is packing for college with her high-school boyfriend in tow, my parents' hopes have been more than met.

By everyone except me.

How are they all so *sure*? Why is everyone else able to find their footing on solid ground?

"I think I'm making a mess of the trip," I whisper to Liam.

He squeezes my shoulder. "We should do something fun while we're in Nafplio. Make you feel better. Maybe something off the bucket list?"

I swipe the edge of my tongue against my teeth, trying not to let the panic show in my eyes. Because of course I've been doing the bucket list. With someone else. And lying about it.

I want to tell him the truth. *I've already been on a boat, but I'm still so down to go on one. It hasn't really happened until it's happened with you.* But the words clog in my throat, tangled in the usual net of fear woven by my ever-present overthinking.

"Yes, please," I say instead. "I really want to spend more time together the rest of the trip."

I'm not lying. Not really. That much feels like the truest thing I've ever said.

He gives me an easy smile, and I return it. But I'm still left with the nauseating feeling that we're not all the way okay.

Our hopes of sneaking off that evening are dashed when Ms. Barlowe announces when we reach our hotel that we'll be spending the rest of the afternoon preparing for the decathlon debate, which will happen after dinner.

"The topic up for discussion is *Can Odysseus be considered a hero?*" Ms. Barlowe tells us. "You'll have the afternoon to prepare with your teams." She rattles two teams off the roster. I find myself partnered with Bodhi and Amalia on the pro side, opposite Liam, who's been assigned to the opposing team. I try not to read into this as we split for the afternoon to prepare for our face-off this evening. Amalia leads Bodhi and me to one of the hotel's conference rooms, a cramped space that still manages to feel huge, with its windows giving us a view of the water stretching past the city. Bodhi and I pause to stare, taking in the sparkling blue of the water framed by the greenery bursting around the city.

"We don't have time to appreciate Greece," Amalia says from the seat she's taken at the circular table crammed into the center of the room. "We have to win this."

"The way the points are broken down, the only thing we have to win is the projects piece," Bodhi reminds her as he takes a seat opposite her at the table. "The rest is just for fun. Or academic enrichment or whatever these fellowship people want to call it."

The truth of his words rings loud in my ears. In the end, it all comes down to our projects, and in my case, I still have nothing but blank pages and whistling emptiness in my brain.

"All the same," Amalia says, primly rearranging the notebooks in front of her, "I'd like to win."

I tear myself away from the window and join them at the table. At the very least, this is my chance to prove that I can hang with the upperclassmen. Be their academic equal.

Of course, the next few hours prove the exact opposite. Amalia, the undisputed group leader, assigns us all reading. Bodhi and Amalia soon have pages of notes filled with meticulous points about how heroic Odysseus is. I have half a page, most of it phrased somewhat sarcastically. I belong on the other team, where they're no doubt roasting him for how much he cheats on his wife over the course of his journey or how he is the only one of his crew who survives. Go down with the ship, Odysseus does not.

"But he also does more to save them than anyone else," I add when Amalia vocalizes this same thought. "Takes more risks, comes up with more escape ideas."

"That's a good point." Amalia nods. "Okay, you're in charge of rebuttals."

The responsibility of this sends the brain gremlin ablaze, but I do my best to breathe through its tap dance and focus on how I can shoot down any point the opposition might bring to the table. The three of us barely notice when the sunset turns the world gold or when the light outside recedes entirely into a summer night, until Ms. Barlowe taps on our conference-room door.

"We're ready for you," she calls.

Bodhi and I exchange nervous looks as Amalia bounces out the door. It's a relief to know he's as trepidatious about this as I am. Not that I'd wish anxiety on anyone, but knowing I'm not alone makes following him back to the lobby a little easier.

Ms. Barlowe gathers us all in another conference room. This one has a tourist-oriented ocean theme, complete with blue-striped walls and large curled seashells glued down to the thick wooden shelves nailed in floating patterns to the wall. The other team is already gathered on one side of the table, so I slide into a seat next to Bodhi on the other side. I fiddle with my pages of notes, hoping to possess some of the quiet self-assuredness Amalia is projecting right now. I'm sure I look more like a nervous third grader playing with the class fidget box.

Ms. Galanis and Ms. Barlowe settle in the front of the room, their now-familiar clipboards propped in front of them, thin wooden reminders that we're being judged on our performance here. That the fellowship will hear about how we do. That, even in a small way, five thousand dollars of life-changing money hang in the balance.

Amalia delivers our opening statement, and I'm impressed with her improv skills. Part of the challenge is that we weren't given much time to prepare, but she delivers our hastily scrawled statement with all the poise and grace of someone who's had weeks to rehearse. Bodhi and I applaud when she finishes, and she shoots us a quick smile that eases the usually tight lines of her face.

George introduces the other team's arguments, and he and Amalia exchange tense looks as they trade places at the front of the room, behind the chair that's serving as our podium. As George talks, I try to catch Liam's eye, but he's focused on the papers in front of him, mouthing the words he'll soon be reciting for the group. Even though he's sitting opposite me, I quietly wish him good luck when it's his turn to stand. But then he starts talking, and my heart sinks. The focus of his speech is on the fate of the crew, and he talks at length about how Odysseus let the members of his team down—literally to the underworld.

Amalia elbows me in the arm, shooting me a sly grin. I give her a panicked look back.

"You got this," she mouths, the corners of her lips curved into a killer smile.

And under her supportive but watchful gaze, I have no choice but to stand up with my rebuttal statement neatly handwritten in front of me.

"It's easy to judge the outcomes without considering the weight of the danger that all these men knowingly signed up for," I begin, my voice shaky as Liam returns to his seat. "But even with that danger, Odysseus took on more than any other in his efforts to keep not just himself but the group alive and well on their journey home."

I keep talking, my voice ramping up in speed and pitch as my nerves get the better of me. I'm not winning any points for presentation, but I catch Ms. Barlowe smiling and nodding as she scribbles onto her clipboard, and Ms. Galanis eyes me with admiration as I career into my closing arguments. When I finish, I don't dare meet Liam's eye.

"That was very well-done from all of you," Ms. Barlowe says, rising when Lucy finishes her team's closing arguments. "We're very impressed with how well you did, especially given the short prep time you had. Congratulations to all. Our winners are Amalia, Bodhi, and Natalie."

I can't help the sharp intake of breath that gasps through my lips. I won something?

Granted, this was a team event, so the credit can't fall squarely on my shoulders, but I can't deny, as Amalia wraps her arms around my shoulders in a celebratory hug, that it feels good to be acknowledged for something.

Until I turn to the opposite side of the table and catch the disappointment in Liam's eyes. I know it's ridiculous to feel guilty for winning, but today was supposed to be about making things right with him.

Instead, I've managed to dig the hole a little deeper.

CHAPTER FOURTEEN

MS. BARLOWE IS MAKING US SPEND the entire day in the library.

"You've had enough 'rotting on the beach' time," she insists when Lucy attempts a puppy-dog look.

In truth, it doesn't take much forcing. As soon as we're all settled at our worktables, books and laptops scattered over the surfaces, we're in our element.

Melanie has taken the morning off to visit cousins in Nafplio, probably because watching us flip pages for hours straight bears little possibility for an interesting day. I'm glad about it. Which probably means all my fears are right, and we're not meant to be. Or that I'm just not meant for love. How else could I be relieved that I don't have to spend the day figuring out how to balance time with her and time with Liam?

Instead, I can sit next to him in easy silence without having to overthink what I'm doing. He's typing up the poems he's scribbled into his notebook at all our sites, and I'm uploading the photos I've been taking to my computer, more for the semblance of productivity than anything else. I stare at the blue line marking the upload's progress. Even though Melanie's not here, my mind is still torn between her and Liam, fixating on the relief in my gut like it's a scab that might be hiding infection.

I glance at Liam to make sure he's focused on his project, and then I turn the brightness down on my computer so he can't read what's on my screen if he happens to glance over. Moving my fingers quietly on the keyboard, I look up classic love stories.

I'm inundated with my favorite stories from ancient Greek mythology. Part of what I love about them is how messy their takes on love are. There isn't one straightforward love story in the bunch. It's part of why Artemis is my favorite too. No love for her. Just frolicking in the woods with a bunch of sworn single ladies forever. Where can I sign up?

But anywhere else I look, all I see is picture-perfect relationships. The stuff of rom-coms, where a third-act breakup is just a bump on the relentless road to happily ever after. The stuff of social media feeds, where everyone is madly in love forever, all traces of past failed loves carefully scrubbed from the archive. What I have with Melanie can't possibly measure up to that. Sure, our first few weeks together have been beautiful. But we're living them out in literal paradise. There's simply no way it's enough to power a lasting relationship.

How is everyone so *sure*?

"How's it going?" Liam asks, jerking me out of my thought spiral. I jump, reflexively command-*W*-ing to close the tab I was reading. He snorts. "Deleting your search history?"

"No," I squeak. "Just done with that article."

He narrows his eyes at me. "You're being weird."

"I'm being so normal."

"You sure?" he says, his eyes reading mine.

I nod, not trusting myself to speak, and his eyebrows tighten. He can see right through me. He knows. I'm sure of it.

"Melanie and I went on a boat ride together."

The words, propelled by the worry soaking in my veins, come spilling out of my mouth before I can stop them.

He blinks at me. "Huh?"

"Melanie asked if I wanted to go on a boat ride, and that was something on our bucket list, and we were supposed to do it together, so I'm sorry I did it with her instead." I'm talking way too fast, the words crowding against my lips. I force myself to meet his gaze, desperate to read his expression.

"What are you talking about?" he asks.

I wince. "Our bucket list."

He closes his notebook, its inky pages slowly flipping shut, and sets it on the table in front of him. "Why didn't you just tell me?"

"I wanted to," I say quickly.

"But then . . ." He trails off, looking at me expectantly. I stare back at him, wide-eyed. My brain is racing faster than my heart, but even with all that work, it still can't seem to string together a coherent sentence.

"I was just so caught up with Melanie, and I didn't want to blow her off because I'd already ditched her, and—"

"No, I'm not mad about the stupid bucket list," Liam says, his eye roll heavy in his tone. "I just don't get why you've been hiding stuff from me all summer."

"What, so I have to report all my movements to you?" I snap, knowing as I do that this is unfair. But his words whip up a defensiveness that comes frothing out of me. He knows how hard dating is for me. We've certainly spent enough nights commiserating over the same pint of Ben & Jerry's Phish Food for him to know what I'm up against here. Or at least know most of it. Isn't it fair enough to need a little space?

"No, not *report*," Liam says, his voice climbing. Lucy and Amalia glance over at our table and exchange looks. I shrink into the back of my chair as Liam goes on. "It just seems like you've been going out of your way to lie to me and hide stuff from me for absolutely no reason."

"No reason?" His words strike me hard in the chest. An admission that, during all the times I've told him how it feels to be trapped in this cycle of questioning everything, of overthinking myself against an unforgiving grindstone, he hasn't really heard me. Because, yes, I've made mistakes. But they've never been for *no reason*.

All eyes in the cohort are on me, but I've never felt more alone.

"I always thought we could tell each other anything," Liam says.

"Doesn't mean we'll always listen, though, it seems," I snap back.

He leans away from me, so much so that his chair tilts onto its back legs. The shock and hurt are so apparent on his face, I want to run from the sight.

"Well, if that's how you feel," Liam says. The front legs of his chair slam onto the floor as he scoops up his things and shoves them into his bag. "Maybe we just need a bit of space."

"Maybe," I say, trying to project as unbothered an aura as I can. His words kill me all the same. Space from him is the last thing I want. All I want is to heal this rift, bring us closer. But he's hitting the eject button before I have a chance to. I can't exactly stop him from walking away.

So I let him. He storms out of the library, leaving me to stare after him in the resounding silence that follows.

Melanie finds me on the beach. An increasingly likely place for me to be.

She hits the sand next to me and joins me in the activity I've been indulging in since nightfall: staring at the waves and wondering why I am Like This. The waning moon reflects on the crest of each wave, lighting up a new thought for me to contemplate.

"I heard what happened," she says softly.

"Lucy loves to share," I mutter.

"I'm here if you need me," Melanie says, laying a hand on my upper arm. Her touch is so gentle, it makes me want to cry. It makes me want to lean into it, to let her take care of me right now.

But it's not built to last, what's between us. There's simply no way it is. So why let myself lean on her now, when I know I'll only fall over later down the line when she's not there anymore?

It's probably time I learned to stand on my own two feet. The way I've been saying I will this whole time. No romance needed.

"I'm all good," I tell her instead.

She leans forward, trying to meet my eye. I don't let my sight drift from the waves. They crash forward, relentless, the next one queued up before the first one has even finished moving across the sand. It's like seeing into my brain, watching the waves of worry that I always know are coming, that are always jockeying in line, waiting for their turn to rush over the shore and reshape the scenery in their image.

"That can't possibly be true," Melanie says.

"I think it is." I turn my head to meet her gaze. A huge mistake. Her brown eyes are so soft, so full of care, that they're enough to waver my resolve for a moment.

But I know what I have to do.

I'm not meant for love. I'm not built to handle it. That's

for everyone else—those who walk so surely toward the people they've chosen, doubt never flickering in their minds. I'm built on doubt, on questions and worries that crash unrelentingly through me in an endless series.

"I don't think we should see each other anymore," I say softly.

Melanie leans away from me in shock. Lot of that going around today. Her eyes flicker over my face as she takes in my words, like she's reading a page of a book.

The silence extends between us, but we don't take our eyes off each other. There's so much I wish I could speak into this moment: *I'm sorry. You're better off this way. Just trust me.*

I can't bring myself to say any of it.

"If that's what you want," she says finally.

It's not.

"It is."

"Then . . ." She gets up, dusting sand off her shorts. "Then I guess I should leave you to it. Give you your space."

She says *space* like it's a dirty word. I turn back to the sea, listening to the sand muffle her footsteps until they disappear.

It's not until I'm safely ensconced in silence that I let the first tears spill. I'm itching to call my mom, like I'm five years old and need a kiss and a Band-Aid for my scraped knee. But I know what she'll say without my asking. She'll remind me that love is worth fighting for—just look at her and Dad all these years later, just look at Lizzie and Andrea and how happy they are. I don't need another reminder that I'm fundamentally broken.

So I wipe my eyes with the back of my hand and let the waves keep crashing forward into the night.

To: Nancy Barlowe; Elena Galanis
Cc: classics2026
From: Jackie Filsinger
Subject: Decathlon Rankings

Dear Maple Grove High School Classics Cohort,

We hope you're enjoying your tour of Greece! Attached are the current point totals for the Greece Through an Ancient Lens Tour Summer Decathlon. Congratulations to all on your incredible progress in these events and on your work on your final projects.

This is your reminder that final projects are due by the last day of your tour. They are to be submitted here before your scheduled flight departure. Judges appointed by the institute will review your projects and announce a winner by the end of the following week.

Feel free to reach out if you have any questions, and enjoy the rest of your tour!

Warmly,
Jackie Filsinger
School Liaison
Stephen Goddard Research Institute

Chapter Fifteen

MS. BARLOWE IS SO EXCITED ABOUT our dinner plans that I feel guilty for the amount of tension hanging heavily in the warm summer air above our group as we make our way to the taverna she's rented out for the evening.

"It's trivia night," she crows as we all take our seats in the pairs she's assigned. Mercifully, I was instructed to sit at a table with Lucy, who is the closest thing I still have to a friendly face in all this mess. I rest my elbows on the sticky plastic covering the blue-and-white checkered tablecloth, my chin buried in my cupped palms.

Ms. Barlowe and Ms. Galanis set themselves up at a long table stretched out toward the back of the room, in front of the door to the kitchen. They have their usual clipboards in front of them, pens clicked and at the ready to judge us. Liam sits as far as possible from me with Amalia, George, and

Henry settled between us. Bodhi, as the front-runner, has been paired with Melanie, who was once again called upon to even out the numbers.

Ms. Galanis comes around to give each team a whiteboard and Expo marker as Ms. Barlowe explains the rules.

"I'll read out the question, and you'll have thirty seconds to write your answer on the board. Every correct answer is worth one point. The first pair to get to ten points wins."

Simple enough, yet the tension that ropes through the room makes it feel impossible to proceed. The partnerships seem intentional enough that I wonder, with embarrassment, how much Ms. Barlowe is tuned into our drama. She's either seen enough to keep me away from Liam and Amalia away from George, or she's the luckiest partner-maker on the planet.

"Let's begin with the first question." Ms. Barlowe turns to Ms. Galanis, who returns to their table at the front of the room with a deck of index cards in tow.

"Which epic hero was the son of Peleus?" she reads off the first card.

Lucy and I give each other a nod, and she pulls the whiteboard toward her to write *Achilles* in her neat handwriting. Ms. Barlowe's timer goes off, and we all hold up our boards, starting the game with an even tie.

"I think speed should count," George calls from his table.

Ms. Barlowe gives him a stern look. "I'm not afraid to institute my rule from my days teaching elementary school. Anyone who argues with me about points will lose a point."

George leans back in his chair immediately.

"But that said, speed will count in the lightning-round tie-breaker, should we need it," Ms. Barlowe assures him as Ms. Galanis readies herself to read the next question.

Between rounds, the taverna staff brings out steaming plates of food. We're soon alternating between writing our answers on the board and sharing plates of pastitsio. The warmth of the pasta spiced with a tender meat sauce should comfort me more than it does. But all I can focus on is the distance between Liam and me.

I keep trying to catch his eye between questions, but he stares steadfastly forward, as if I don't even exist. I shrivel under the lack of his gaze. Without Liam, I'm not sure how to *be*.

So I gorge myself on more pastitsio, hoping the warmth it offers will help.

"What social phenomenon derives its name from *ostracon*, or *pottery shards*?" Ms. Galanis asks.

Lucy looks at me with blank eyes, but I know this one. It's one of Liam's favorite fun facts.

"That's right," Ms. Barlowe says, nodding at my board as her eyes sweep the room at the end of the round. "*Ostracism*, named for the pottery shards used in the ancient Athenian voting process to cast out a member of the community for ten years by popular vote."

It's a question that suddenly feels oddly pointed. We're all doing a pretty good job of voting one another off the island these days. The extremity of our emotions, all clashing against one another, feels overwhelming. I think back to my anger at Liam in the library yesterday over the idea that I'd done this all for no reason. Of course I had a reason.

We all do, I realize. Everyone here is reacting to their internal shit as much as the situation around them. During this summer, all of us are lit matches being met with fuel.

I just wish I knew how to douse the flames.

Given that I have no friends and no girlfriend and nothing but my starring role as the focal point of the cohort's new gossip train, it's easy to focus on my project this morning. In fact, I'm so inspired that I beg Ms. Barlowe to let me skip today's outing so I can keep working.

The truth is that I'm much more inspired by the idea of being alone, far away from anyone in the cohort, than I am by my project. But it gets her to say yes.

So I pretend to sleep in as Amalia gets ready for the day, and I don't even leave our hotel room until an hour after the bus was scheduled to depart. I burrito myself deeper into the fluffy duvet, even though it's way too hot to indulge in blankets, and I don't emerge until I can feel a bead of sweat dripping down my spine.

I shower off the sweat and head to the hotel pool, where I'm sure I'll find lots of inspiration for my project, should Ms. Barlowe ask what I was doing there. The other hotel guests must be out sightseeing too, because I find the little pool mercifully empty. It's nestled in the hotel's picturesque courtyard. I'm surrounded by plants, the sweet scent of the jasmine climbing the white wooden fence around the cobble-stoned area flavoring the air. I glide into the water and let myself float across the surface, closing my eyes as the sunlight fans across my face.

And to give myself some credit, I do think about my project. I certainly don't want to think about anything else that's going on in my life right now. My friendships, my love life, my family . . . It's all grim at the moment. At least I can do something about my project.

Hypothetically.

I dunk myself underwater, enjoying the humming silence. I've always loved the way water dulls the edges of all my senses. It almost does the same to my thoughts. At least now they're ringing with all the pieces I have for my project. The endless photos. The random snippets of information I've scribbled as I pretended to be busy during our tours. The stories I love.

I break the surface of the water, sputtering. A half idea has finally come to me. I heave myself out of the pool, the smell of chlorine clinging to my skin as I wrap myself tight in a towel and drop onto a lounge chair.

I can put together a virtual museum exhibit focused on the relationship between the ancient world and our lives. It's been the through line of the summer. Not just in the photos

I've taken of ancient sites nestled within the bustle of modern streets, but in the echoes of the myths I feel in my own present dramas. I prop my laptop open across my thighs and start brainstorming a list of ideas. I can use the photos to make virtual display pieces and link each of them to a story. Andrea is gearing up to be a computer scientist, and I'm sure I could get her to help me with codifying my design. I just have to come up with the visuals and write the pieces to link them all together.

I'm so excited that I actually open my text app to send an excited message to Liam, or Melanie, or even the cohort group chat. I finally have an idea!

And then, embarrassingly, I remember that I have no friends at the moment. I'm entirely, soul-crushingly alone.

I sit back in the lounge chair, staring past my computer screen into the void beyond. The shimmering blue of the pool blurs in my vision. There has to be someone in this world I can talk to.

I blink, and the world refocuses.

Still dripping water from my fingertips, I click over to Paige's name. It's been a while since I've texted her, and our message history is buried under all my more frequent-flier texting friends.

> **NATALIE:** hi Paige. Any chance I can take you up on that emergency session offer?

There's nothing to do now but wait for her to respond. And keep working on my project.

So I do.

"It's nice to see you."

Paige is, by all accounts, *way* too happy to see me. She always has a sunny vibe about her, but today it's turned up to a billion. I can feel her anticipation of a breakthrough seeping out of her pores.

"It's nice to see you too," I admit. It's possible I hate on Paige too much. Like, yeah, she's way too chipper. But right now, with my mood in the sewer, it's sort of nice to be reminded that joy still exists in the world.

"So, how's the trip going?" Paige asks, leaning toward her camera. "What prompted you to reach out to me?"

I sigh, shifting on the rickety chair by the desk in my hotel room. I'm freshly showered, my hair still wrapped tightly in a bath towel to stop it from dripping onto the shoulders of the ancient band T-shirt I stole from my dad to use as pajamas. Nothing about me screams mental wellness.

"I'm having a struggle," I tell her.

"What with?" she asks.

"Well." I take a deep breath. "I met a girl, and we sort of started dating, but then I freaked out and broke up with her and also had a huge, possibly friendship-ending fight with Liam, and also I think I fundamentally don't belong in my family."

I stare into the camera at Paige, daring her to respond. She nods slowly, and I brace myself for some therapy-speak that's just going to make me feel even more alienated from humanity at large.

She tilts her head to one side. "So, an idyllic Greek paradise, then."

A snort of laughter tears out of my surprised throat. "You could put it that way."

"That sounds hard," Paige says, turning serious. "I'm glad you reached out."

"Same," I admit. Even saying everything out loud has made me feel lighter. Like someone else has picked up the other side of my baggage, and we can walk together for a little while.

"Do you want to tell me more about what happened?" Paige offers, and I nod. "Where do you want to start?"

So I fill her in on the "dog chasing its tail" thoughts that led me to end things with Melanie before they could even really get going and the fight with Liam that happened on the way.

"Oof," Paige says. "It sounds like those intrusive thoughts have really been messing with the trip."

The phrase *intrusive thoughts* bumps against me, and I suppress a wince.

"I don't know. I've been having a hard time with, like, OCD as a concept," I tell her. "I don't think it applies to me."

"Which is exactly why I don't prioritize diagnoses," Paige says. It's not the first time she's explained this to me, but if I'm honest, I wasn't super listening last time. Denial just seemed safer than auditory processing. "I'm not here to label you. I mean, it's something I have to do for insurance paperwork, but in our sessions, it's not something that's at the front of my mind. Or even really in the back of it."

"So, what, then?" I ask.

"Believe it or not, I'm here for *you*," she says with a smile. "I'm not labeling you, because I don't believe in putting you in a box and using its parameters to define you. I want to get to know who you are as a person and teach you the tools you can use to deal with the ways your symptoms are affecting your life."

A lump forms in my throat. Making space to acknowledge the way the endless spiral of intrusive thoughts is ruining my life without letting it define me sounds . . . too good to be true.

And yet it's exactly what she's been offering this entire time. Hope.

Why have I been running away, screaming, with both hands over my ears?

"That sounds nice," I admit. Then I wrinkle my nose. "Does that mean more exposure-response prevention?"

Because, right. That's why I ran away. She wanted me to face my fears *without trying to make myself feel better*. Like, hello? How?

"It can," Paige says with a small laugh, "but I'm not going to force you into anything you're not comfortable with. You're allowed to say no to me."

I raise my eyebrows. Saying no to my therapist had not occurred to me before.

"Do you think it would help?" I ask cautiously.

"It can be very effective," Paige says. "But I think we should focus on getting through this moment first. It sounds like it's been an intense time."

"You could say that," I mutter.

"I will say that," Paige says with a smile. "You're dealing with a lot right now, and it's the kind of struggle no one else can see is happening, so I completely understand feeling alone."

I swallow thickly again. Who knew therapy could be this validating?

"I've still messed up, though," I say quietly.

"Let's focus on what you can do moving forward, then," Paige says. "What are the parts you can control? What do you think you can do to make things right?"

The problem is, even though I spend the next half hour reflecting on all the ways I've wronged my friends, I still have no idea how to fix them.

CHAPTER SIXTEEN

I SUCCESSFULLY MANAGE TO STAY ALONE during the entire drive to Olympia and the "checking into the hotel" process. I'm assigned to share a room with Amalia again, which makes this easy. We're both so immersed in our projects that the only sound filling our hotel room is our respective typing—mine a slow pecking and hers an aggressive waterfall of key smashing.

So it's not until the next morning, when we're all filing off the bus and onto our tour of the site of the first Olympics, that I realize how much tension has permeated the entire cohort. It's definitely not just me having an *intense time* this trip. Everyone is paired off or standing conspicuously alone. Liam stands near Lucy but not close enough that they could have a conversation. I wonder if they've had a fight too. Not knowing what's going on with him gnaws at my insides.

The worst is Melanie, though. She's hanging out by her mom, staring at the dust blowing around her sneakers.

Ms. Galanis starts the tour, explaining the history of the games as we walk past the ruined marble structures where the games were first held. The now-familiar sight of ancient columns line both sides of the grassy pathway we walk down, until we reach a long stretch of dirt carved into the ground.

"But, as I hope you've learned over the course of this trip," Ms. Galanis says, "these stories are still very much alive around us. We still have the Olympics in our present world, obviously. And today we'll be having our own."

She gestures to the ancient racetrack in front of us, and we all exchange glances in spite of ourselves. What does she mean?

"We're going to hold our very own Olympics right here, on the same land where ancient Greek athletes raced one another thousands of years ago," Ms. Galanis says. "These Olympics are the last event in our decathlon."

We all pointedly don't exchange glances with one another. The last thing we need is to introduce more competitive edginess to our circle right now. Can our teachers really not read the room?

Or maybe they're reading it too well and are somehow thinking of this as a team-building activity that's going to save us all. In which case, they are sorely mistaken.

"Let's start with shot put," Ms. Barlowe says, pulling two bocce balls out of her massive purse. She hands one to Bodhi and one to Lucy.

They exchange glances as they file toward the line Ms. Galanis draws in the sand.

Bodhi is not, strictly speaking, involved in any of the drama, but he's always tacitly disapproved of how willing Lucy is to throw herself into mixes she, too, is not technically part of. Lucy has always read this as high-horsey of him.

They both fling their bocce balls, and Bodhi wins handily.

An awkward shuffle passes through the group as we all shift our weight, looking at the columns and the dirt and the trees and everywhere but one another's faces.

"All right, next up we have the long jump," Ms. Galanis says, "with Amalia and George."

She tells them that they'll just be jumping as far as they can from the starting line, which seems ridiculous to me. We're here because we're the nerdiest people alive. Why make us lean into our athletic sides with made-up sports when no one is speaking and everyone just wants to hide behind their projects and work in silence?

George winks at Amalia as they line up next to each other. He jumps first, landing tragically close to where he started. Amalia jumps after him, landing exactly on top of him. They both topple to the ground.

We all freeze, and I wonder if the rest of the cohort is sharing my first thought—that Amalia has somehow decided to physically attack George in front of both our teachers.

But then we hear their laughter ringing from the cloud of dust that's engulfed them. I breathe a sigh of relief, but it's immediately replaced by confusion.

And then, as they're getting up, Amalia kisses George on the cheek. In front of all of us.

Lucy screams, "Oh my god. Oh my god. Oh my god. You guys are dating. Oh my god."

We're all frozen, staring at them in shock. After all the drama we've borne witness to, they've been secretly dating this whole time?

Amalia nods, lacing her fingers in George's hand. I hold my breath, glancing at Lucy. She's been so close to Amalia for so long, I wouldn't be surprised if she's furious. The cohort is about to explode in all new ways.

Lucy screams again, and I brace myself for the onslaught. But then she's jumping up and down and running over to throw her arms around both of them.

"I'm so glad," she says. I can tell from George's vaguely purple expression that she's squeezing his neck way too hard. "I always said you were made for each other."

"Plagiarism aside," Amalia says playfully.

"I literally never plagiarized, you slanderous liar," George quips back.

Watching them joke about this feels like watching a dog do backflips. They're still holding hands when they get back to the group, and it's a sight I'll never get used to.

But before any of us can press them for details, Ms. Barlowe waves me forward.

"Okay," Ms. Galanis says, shaking her head. "Up next for a hopefully much less eventful footrace, we have Natalie versus Melanie."

I want to crawl into a hole and lie there forever. In my worst nightmares, I'd never imagined they would do this to me.

I drag my feet to the starting line, dust clouding around my sneakers with every step I refuse to pick up off the ground. I reach the starting line eventually in spite of my best efforts. Melanie and I keep our eyes straight ahead, and the palpable tension between us feels like a slap.

At least I'm fast. This will be over quickly.

Ms. Barlowe counts us in, and I take off as soon as she says "Go." For the first few seconds, all I can feel is the air rushing through my lungs, the pounding of my sneakers against the hard dirt. Running always clears my head like nothing else.

So maybe that's why it takes right now for me to realize, truly, what I've put Melanie through this summer.

She's easily become one of my favorite people. She's met the ridiculous conditions I set at the beginning of the trip, the ones that were only in place because they were impossible. And all I've done is doubt her.

It's so unfair. More than unfair. I owe her a million apologies.

And I owe myself more than what I've been giving too. A second chance at therapy, at love, at friendship—at the things I've withheld because I thought I failed when my first relationship ended when I was fourteen years old.

I take a deep breath and decide, just for this moment, to trust myself.

I slow my steps. Behind me, a cheer erupts from the group, and I recognize Lucy's voice. Of course she's the first one to realize what I'm doing. Her whooping lets the rest of the cohort in on it, and soon they're all cheering and chanting as I screech from a sprint to a jog, letting Melanie take the lead. Take the race. Take the prize.

She wins, and I jog up behind her with a smile on my face. She narrows her eyes at me. "You let that happen."

"I did," I admit.

"I don't need your pity-race-throwing," she says, rolling her eyes.

"That's not—"

"I know," she says with a smile. "Lucy told me about your stupid bet after you ended things."

I shrug, a half smile playing on my lips. "I met someone who made me feel at home while showing me new places, and who made me feel like myself while pushing me to grow. I was never gonna meet someone who could beat me in a race without some help."

Melanie meets my eyes, and I can see the questions hanging heavy around her irises.

"I'm so sorry for this summer," I tell her. "I have a lot of reasons for why I'm like this, but no excuses. It was so wrong to drag you into my mess before I was ready to treat you with the care and consideration you deserve, and I'm really sorry."

Melanie nods slowly. "I appreciate that a lot. And I'm sorry too. For letting my anxiety lead my way. I shouldn't have tried to pressure you into a relationship you didn't feel ready for. Friends?"

She holds out a hand, and it's easy to take it.

"Friends," I agree.

Friendship isn't everything I want from her. I can see clearly enough that I realize that now, wholly and completely. But after everything we've been through this summer—all the mistakes I've made—I'm grateful that she's offering it.

It's not everything I want, but getting to keep her in my life—it's enough.

"I saw what you did."

I startle, looking up from my laptop screen. I've been so tuned into my designs for my museum exhibit that I didn't even hear Liam slip through the door to our hotel room that Amalia had left ajar because she keeps losing her key.

I close my laptop and push it to the other side of my bed, making space for him to sit by me.

"Which part?" I ask.

"Letting Melanie win that race," he says with a grin. "I'm assuming it means you're sorting through things?"

I nod, staring down at the white detailing on the edge of the sheets. "Yeah. I'm really sorry about . . . everything this summer."

"Me too," he says. "Things got weird."

"I made them weird," I say with a little laugh.

He lowers himself onto the bed, crossing his legs underneath him.

"But I get what you meant about having reasons."

"Not excuses, though," I admit. "I was leaning on them too hard to justify my behavior to myself, and I'm really sorry."

"Well, I'm sorry for not being more understanding," Liam says.

"I know you were trying to help," I tell him. "It just hit a nerve. The pressure to be in a relationship was part of why I found it so hard to be calm about the idea of one. And then I was getting all this scrutiny from the group, and it sort of made me hit the panic button."

Liam nods. "I get that, and I'm so sorry."

"It's okay," I say. "I know everyone meant well."

"But we should've heard you," Liam says, and I nod quietly.

He reaches over to squeeze my hand. I squish his fingers back, and we sit in silence for a moment. It's a quiet that swells with our mutual relief, both of us glad that we're okay again. That the world has returned to its normal axis.

"Can you believe Amalia and George have been dating this whole time?" I say after a while.

Liam shakes his head. "Lucy pressed Amalia for details and found out they almost broke up at the start of the trip, and that's why things got so weird."

I tuck my toes under the comforter. "Wild. I do also think the competition put a strain on everyone."

"We'd be so much better off if we could share our

research instead of pitting it against everyone else's ideas," Liam mutters.

"What if we just agreed to spend the prize money on something that benefits the whole group?" I suggest. "We share the research, we work together, and the prize money is just for us as a group. Doesn't matter who wins."

Liam nods slowly. "I like it."

"Let's pitch it to Lucy," I tell him. "She'll get everyone else on board."

He gets up and wraps his arms around me when I do the same. I squeeze his shoulders.

"I'm glad we're okay," he whispers.

I nod as we pull apart. "Me too."

"Love you," he says, and I return the sentiment. Things might still be far from perfect, but at least this one part of the great series of summer disasters of 2026 has been resolved. It's finally the proof I need that I can handle keeping my friends close even while clinging to hopes of romance.

Even though those hopes right now feel further away than ever.

It's been hours since Amalia started filling our hotel room with her quiet snores, but I can't find my way to sleep no matter how many times I toss against the firm mattress of this hotel bed. My session with Paige keeps replaying in my ears. The comfort that came with everything she said about how I'm not defined by my diagnosis now falls flat against my ears as I chase the same thought loops in circles around my own brain.

The neon red lines on the nightstand clock blink 3:17 at me. I'll never get any sleep at this rate. With a frustrated kick, I toss the thin white blanket off me and slip out of the room. The bright lights in the hallway are jarring after so long in the dim peacefulness of the bedroom, and I blink heavily as I make my way down the hall toward the exit.

The cool night breeze feels like a relief after the stifled indoor air of the bedroom. I make my way across the courtyard, my sneaker steps feeling loud against the silence of the deep night. The moon has reduced to a curved sliver, leaving space for the stars to light up the sky. I settle on one of the lounge chairs by the pool, breathing in deep the scent of jasmine and tracing the constellations with my eyes. All the ones I find tie back to the stories told by the ancients, stories that we still echo today.

As always, it's a comforting thought. It reminds me that there are more than just stories of struggles with love that have lasted through the ages. There are family feuds, clashes in decades-long friendships, and enough mother-daughter drama to fuel centuries of storytelling.

It gives me enough strength to pull out my phone and dial my mom.

"Hi, honey," she says when she answers. "I'm at a fitting with Lizzie. Isn't it late where you are?"

"I couldn't sleep," I say, my voice breaking at the sound of hers. I hadn't realized, until I heard Paige say it, how much the idea of being labeled had been weighing on me.

And how much of that came from my parents. From their well-meaning but overwhelming worry.

"You should talk to Paige about it," Mom says lightly, which gives me the perfect segue into what I was hoping to talk to her about.

"I talked to Paige," I admit. "It helped."

"That's so great, sweets," Mom says. I can hear the pride bubbling in her voice. "She's an incredible resource. You should—"

"But I also think it would help if we could talk about her less?" I say, my heart burning against my rib cage as I force the words out. "She says I'm not just my OCD label. That she barely even cares about it. But sometimes it feels like that's the only thing you see now."

My hands shake at the weight of spilling all these feelings out loud. But at the same time, I sort of can't wait to tell Paige later that I found the strength to do it.

Mom is quiet on the other end of the line for a moment, long enough that my worry starts to spike up again. Is she going to be furious?

But then she sighs, her breath crackling on the line between us. "I'm so sorry, Nat. I've been worried about you, but I know you're much more than what you're dealing with. I love you so much."

It's a simple three sentences, but they bring with them all

the relief I needed. My shoulders unwind, and I lean back into the lounge chair, staring up at the stars.

"Let's hear about your trip, then," Mom says.

"Don't you have to help Lizzie?" I croak.

"I have some time," Mom says.

So under the canopy of stars and jasmine, I tell her everything that's happened this summer so far.

Chapter Seventeen

IT'S OUR LAST STOP OF THE trip, and the idea that we'll all be home soon makes everything around us feel surreal.

We're spending our last few days in Delphi, once home to the most famous oracle of the ancient world. Lucy has convinced everyone that we should split the prize money no matter who wins, and the vibes in the group already feel smoother. Amalia and George walk, hand in hand, ahead of us, which only makes the surrealness all the more palpable. Bodhi is trying to convince us all to spend the prize money on an art lesson series in the fall, with the new college students joining via video call, and he's persistent enough that even my clumsy fingers are seriously considering it.

Melanie bounces around the group, chatting with every-one. It's the only sadness left. She's become such a part of the group that it's hard to imagine leaving her in Greece when the rest of us pack ourselves onto our plane home.

The ruins at Delphi are a temple dedicated to Apollo, so I bury my feelings in photographing finds related to Artemis's twin.

After a tour of the archaeological museum, where I spend way too long obsessing over the bronze chariot driver, Ms. Barlowe releases us to explore the grounds. They're split between several key sites. I'm torn between wanting to spend these last few days hanging out with Melanie and stinging a little at the knowledge that I threw away the opportunity to spend our remaining time kissing her. In the end, I venture alone down the grassy hill to the marble remains of the Temple of Apollo, close to where the Oracle at Delphi would have delivered her advice.

I wish she were still here, I think as I sit on what's left of the temple's marble steps. At this point, I would take the advice of a woman breathing in vapors from a chasm in the mountain. Anything seems to be better than the inner workings of my single brain cell.

I've made such a mess of this summer. And even though things are better with Liam, I so regret the precious time I wasted panicking over nothing instead of enjoying the trip and what could've been a delightful summer romance with Melanie. Instead, I've ended up alone on a pile of ancient rocks, yearning for the advice of the Pythia. Ancient rulers came to her to avoid calamities, and I sure could use a road map on how to get around disasters of my own making.

I'm brought out of my thoughts by a footfall behind me, and I turn to see Melanie walking toward me. She grins as she sits on the steps next to me.

"Contemplating the future?" she asks, nodding toward the ancient path to the oracle.

"You laugh, but, yeah, pretty much," I tell her.

"What's on your mind?" she asks.

I glance at her. She's staring at me, her wide brown eyes flicking over my face. I have no idea how honest I'm allowed to be.

But hiding my feelings has not served me well this summer. I take a deep breath and decide to make Paige, if no one else, proud.

"Honestly, I feel like I've royally screwed up this summer," I admit. "I regret not being all the way in on us from the start. I should have been."

She blinks twice. The silence between us stretches long, and then too long. Enough that I regret opening my stupid mouth, no matter what Paige will say about it in our next session.

But then Melanie bites a corner of her lower lip, her brow furrowing. "Do you really mean that?"

"Very much," I tell her. "My vision was clouded by all these worries and thought spirals, and I couldn't see us clearly. Which was so unfair to you. And to what could've been. I'm so sorry."

She nods slowly, and then all at once, she reaches out to take my hand. The weight, the warmth of her fingers still feel so right against my palm. Like they belong there. I blink fast to keep the tears from falling.

"It's not too late," she says quietly.

"Isn't it?" I whisper. "I ruined the time we had together."

"You're getting on a plane in a few days, not dying," Melanie says. The laughter in her tone buoys my hopes. Could she really be so willing to forgive all the mistakes I've made?

The grace of it feels almost too much to bear.

"Do you really think we could make it work?" I ask, and she nods. "Are you sure you want to, after everything I—"

I can't finish my sentence, because her lips are against mine before I can make it to the end of my next word. And, well, who am I to argue?

I pull her closer, one hand wrapping around her waist and the other curling into her hair, craving more of her warmth. I can feel her smile against my lips, and I never want to stop kissing.

We finally break apart, but our limbs are still tangled together. We stay that way for a long time, breathing each other in as the afternoon turns to evening around us.

And just now, even I can't find anything here to worry about.

EPILOGUE

NEW YORK CITY IS STICKY HOT in July. The air drips from my skin, and I yearn for the dry heat of Greece last summer.

It doesn't help that I'm standing in Bryant Park in the harsh sun, sweating up a storm with my old cohort around me. All the seniors who graduated last year and came on the trip are back from college, and they've joined for today's special adventure. We jockey to stand in the shade of the thin trees lining the sidewalk, desperate to save ourselves from the sun beating down on the worn concrete underfoot.

Liam did spend his prize money on an art class series for the group, and as a result, we can all do at least decent sketches when we tour museums. But there was just enough left over to treat the group to one more reward.

Although this one feels especially designed for me.

I stand on the tips of my toes, scanning the crowd of people freshly emerged from the nearest subway entrance. And suddenly, after months of late-night calls and texting at odd hours and audio messages about how much we've fallen in love with each other, Melanie is here, lighting up the sidewalk with her smile.

I break away from the cohort and sprint toward her, not stopping until I can crush her against me, until we're one of those horrible couples making out in the middle of the street.

Behind us, the cohort breaks out into a series of boos, but I can hear the laughter behind them. We're both smiling as we break apart, and I gesture to the steps of the public library. It's finally our turn to play tour guide for Melanie, and we don't intend to waste a moment.

Except for the ones we'll be stealing away, just her and me.

"I can't believe you brought me here," Melanie says as she squishes Liam into a hug.

"We all missed you too much," Bodhi says, piling himself into the hug.

"Some more than others," Lucy adds, grinning at me.

I roll my eyes at her, but I also refuse to let go of Melanie's hand, no matter how sweaty we both get.

"Let's get into some AC, shall we?" Liam says, fanning himself with his shirt collar.

"Please," Melanie begs. "I can't believe you all live in this hell swamp."

"I did warn you," I remind her.

"Well, it's worth it," she says, leaning over to kiss me. Liam boos again, but Lucy applauds this time. I treat her to another eye roll as we make our way into the library.

And I can't believe this is my real life. My hand in Melanie's, our time stretching languidly before us, walking between the white marble lions to the first stop of an endless summer we get to spend together.

ACKNOWLEDGMENTS

The making of this book spans the same timeline as my first pregnancy—I wrote my first draft in my first trimester, and finished copyedits in those soft few weeks after my daughter was born. All to say, I've never leaned more heavily on the incredible team of people who have made my books possible, and, as always, I've reached the end of this writing process so grateful for everyone who helped me along it.

Thank you so much to Kelsey Horton for your brilliant insights in developing these characters and this story. I can't believe it's our fourth book together, and I'm so grateful for this journey we've been on! Huge thanks also to Emma Leynse for guiding me through every step of the process.

Hugest shout-out to my agent Penny Moore for making this and all my books happen. I'll always be so grateful for our partnership.

Thank you to the entire team at Random House Children's Books for your work in bringing this book to life. Jeff Östberg, thank you for breathing such gorgeous life into all my book covers. Thank you to Trisha Previte, Cathy Bobak,

Tamar Schwartz, Jamie Johnson, Wendy Loggia, Mallory Loehr, and the entire RHCB marketing and publicity teams.

Behind every book is a group chat running on the perfect balance of encouragement and complaining. Thank you, Sonia Hartl, Annette Christie, Kelsey Rodkey, Marisa Kanter, Evelyn Luchs, Robert Jewell, Jack Filsinger, and Nadja Tiktinsky for keeping me going even when I very much did not want to.

Thank you to Luke and Karen, who will always be my teaching partners no matter where we work, and to our students, who make our work worth doing.

Thank you to Erin for, well, very much everything. I couldn't have made it through this book or this year without you, nor would I ever want to. Darcy, who was with me the whole time I wrote this—thank you for learning how to smile and for sleeping eight hours straight last night, a very cool move.

About the Author

AURIANE DESOMBRE is a middle-school teacher and author of love stories for teens and tweens, including *I Think I Love You, The Sister Split, I Love You S'More,* and *Love in Ruins.* She currently lives in Los Angeles with her wife and daughter, their badly behaved dog, and an ever-growing collection of houseplants (most of which are pretty well behaved).

aurianedesombre.com